The
Cautious Amorist

NORMAN LINDSAY

THE
CAUTIOUS
AMORIST

Illustrated by the
Author

GROSSET & DUNLAP · PUBLISHERS · NEW YORK
by arrangement with Farrar & Rinehart

The
Cautious Amorist

CHAPTER ONE

THE lights had gone out suddenly on the S.S. *Minorca*, and there was a twitter of alarm along the promenade deck, where the passengers lay about in chairs, pleasantly stodged by ozone and overeating.

Voices were raised in tones of annoyed inquiry: the steward's orchestra faltered through a bar and stopped: couples dancing remained posed stiffly in a conventional embrace, like people waiting for a flash-light photo-

3

graph. There were giggles, sounds of protest; somebody fell over a deck chair.

A voice, the purser's, arrived in the dark, distributing reassurances. "It's all right—only a blown fuse. The lights will go on in a moment. . . ." Voices, pitched uneasily, were lowered again, by a pleasant illusion of enlightenment.

Now that light had gone, noses sensed the tang of salt water and the vast wet spaces of the sea. A swift tropic cloudburst passed over the ship, shutting her in to the rails between dimly luminous curtains behind which a low moon was setting. Three days out from Honolulu, they were aware of the warm night, now that the ship had slowed to half speed. Visibility there was none. Therefore, it was in a tone of vague alarm that a voice said suddenly:

"I say, what a bright star!"

Winking in the haze, that bright star swerved suddenly at the ship, and instantly the engine room telephone rang for full speed. A huge bulk rose out of the mist and seemed to swing astern, but before contracted hearts could diagnose their terror the purser's voice went up, distinct with horrified conviction:

"Jesus wept!—Into us!"

The oncoming ship had been put astern too late. She seemed only to graze the *Minorca's* quarter, but there followed a crash of splintered wood and buckled iron that tore a rent to her after hatchway.

A horrible sound in that darkness, which released terror in a wave of dementia. The ship's people rushed

to compete with disaster across decks clogged by sprawling, squalling imbeciles, convinced of an instant knowledge and detestation of death. A bad ten minutes for
everybody while the *Minorca* decided not to sink just
yet, though she gave a belly-quaking lurch and listed
heavily before the water-tight doors shut off the rush
of water to her holds, while the ship that had rammed
her backed slowly into the haze to a hoarse shouting
between bridges.

By that time the boat crews were at their stations,
working swiftly and with precision. The starboard
davits were useless, but the port boats were being swung
out, and all along the boat deck there was a thudding of
dismantled chocks and the creak of tackle. That was
only so much added panic to the mob below, huddled
on a treacherous mass of iron which a hand's push might
send to the bottom.

Carrol had been seated well forward when the lights
went out. He was reading Boswell's *Corsica*, which he
had chanced on in the ship's library, and still held the
book upright, impatient at an annoying interruption.
He saw nothing of the portentous bulk that rushed on
them out of the rain screen, and had fallen to blowing
into his pipe stem to clear it. With that crash aft the
pipe seemed jerked from his mouth by invisible forces
and he grabbed and caught it in mid-air with miraculous
precision.

Confounded by the clamour down the promenade
deck, he continued to sit there inanely while the deck
took a sickening incline to port and there remained. At

that, panic shot him up to slide into a bedlamite scramble of bodies at the rail, where he went down, his pipe still clutched in one hand but Boswell gone overboard. His fingers were trodden on and he swore fiercely till a blow in the ribs winded him, while he levered at a fat woman who had fallen across his legs. The thin fabric of an evening frock ripped at his thrust, a hand that smelt of scented soap was pressed against his face, a body plunged with insensate gambols and a voice screamed incessantly.

Carrol found a rail stanchion and lugged himself up, fighting off clutches from unseen hands. All that was done in a mechanical fury; his thoughts were rushed by the dilemma of terror; a conviction of disaster and a policy to avert it. Policy could think only of getting at a life-belt, and he tried to recall where they were stored, and locate himself in the dark. Life-belts were stored in embrasures on the main deck, he remembered now, and he clawed a passage to the stairway, breathing in gasps. Like a man under a shower. There he collided with an equally breathless steward, and grappled at him.

"W'a's up?" he gasped.

"Run down—boat stations," panted the steward.

He thrust Carrol off and scrambled on. Another burst of screams from the rail as the ship lurched again under the drag of water in her after hold. Carrol remained gripping the stairhead, helpless to move. A horror of being caught below decks in a sinking ship paralyzed him; his thoughts were a blasphemous whirl of hatred for the gods.

Lanterns appeared, and the mob surged towards them, turning tragic masks up to each swinging circle of light; masks that no one had seen on that ship before. Above their clamour an impatient voice shouted:

"Stand clear—there's no danger—stand clear——"

That was the second officer, butting a way through the mob with the informality of a policeman in a crowded street. Behind him a brawny fellow with a sweat rag round his neck held the lantern aloft, fending off the crowd with good-humoured intolerance. "Go easy—it's no more than a bit of a bump from the tramp yonder that's standin' by to take us off. Have sense, now, if you can't have reason. . . ."

A note of derision from this messiah of hope sent a long shiver of relief through the surging heads, and voices twittered, coming down the scale to cover an exhibition of funk that was still busy with them. All wished to get close to that lantern, now lashed to an iron stanchion, where a pilot ladder trailed from the boat deck as with a rattle of gear a boat was run down and launched neatly. Its crew swarmed down the ladder, and two more boats came down on either side. There was a mishap with one of those. By a too sudden release of the falls she hit the water violently, and the emergency ladder, kinked under the oars, jerked them into the water, along with one of the hands at the falls. There was commotion down there for a moment, put in order by the second officer shouting: "Pick up that man; make that boat fast to the ladder, you. Come alongside, you others. Stand by the ladder. Now then——"

The man with the sweat rag had swung back a section of hinged rail at the pilot ladder, and the crowd surged forward. "Stand back," ordered the second officer. He was submerged a moment, to reappear with dramatic effect. There was a smart crack, and the surge was arrested. "I told you to stand back," he added rationally. "Now then, women first."

From his position at the stairhead Carrol could see the crowd packed round the lantern, and the busy movements of the second officer passing a row of women's heads to the man with the sweat rag, who shepherded them onto the ladder. Out in the thinning rain a dim mass sustaining a few blurred lights showed where the other ship waited to pick them up.

Order out of chaos lifted the tension of Carrol's nerves, but he understood that there was need for haste too. Nagged at by a horrid sense of insecurity in the sloping decks he ran down the stairs, and fumbling in the dark, found life-belts in the rack and lugged one down and put it on. It gave him another breathing interval, and he stood by the rail, glancing up at the leaning side of the ship, visible now by lanterns lashed along the upper deck. Boats were in the water, boats were still coming down, and women in summer frocks straggled down the pilot ladders. The boat below him had just filled up, and moved off with a slapping of

oars into the night. Another boat, the one that had dropped in the slings, lay alongside, hitched to the ladder, with only one man aboard. Peering down, the second officer shouted at him,

"Pull that boat in."

"She's no oars," called the man.

"She'll tow. Stand by the ladder."

Carrol moved close to the rail, controlling a desire to drop into the boat, which was only eight feet below him. The man in her was hanging onto the ladder, steadying it, and his face, turned up to the light, was strained with anxiety. Looking up, Carrol saw a girl's figure sway onto the ladder. She came down swiftly, passing a foot from him, and he saw the light flick on her bare arms and flimsy dance frock. With a gasp of relief she dropped into the boat. . . .

At that moment an ordered sequence of events failed Carrol. He felt his stomach lift as the *Minorca* lurched again by another inrush of water somewhere, and screams burst from the promenade deck. That uproar caused Carrol to lose his head by the precise logic of funk. He whipped over the rail, took a grip of the deck stanchion, and dropped, landing on the man in the boat, who was standing on the gunwale. He let out a startled yell, gripped the ladder, and swung off the boat as it slid from under him.

Confused, Carrol scrambled up and grabbed at the ladder, but missed it as the boat sidled out on the swell. Just as well, perhaps; there was a crescendo of panic on the promenade deck. Glancing up, Carrol had an impression of furious faces along the rail and a swirl of figures under the lantern. A woman clung to the ladder screaming. In silhouette, two figures lurched out against the light and dropped with a mighty splash into the water.

Carrol leaped to the side as two heads emerged in a thrashing of arms. "Here," he yelled, and threw the painter. It was gripped, and he tugged hard. An arm shot up and clutched the boat's life-lines.

"Hold on! Here, give me your hand," said Carrol.

"Give a hand to this mudhead that's tryin' to drown me," said the other. It was the man with the sweat rag. The mudhead, so described, had him clutched about the neck. Carrol reached over and with some exertion assisted him, also, to grasp the life-lines. For a moment both hung, ejecting water.

"Wait now, till I get me leg over," said the other. His sweat rag had gone, insignia of his job of stoker. With a powerful heave he dragged himself aboard. "That for drownin'," he said, and spat. The mudhead made a longer job of it, for he was waterlogged, frightened, and naturally ungainly. With the stoker's help he was lugged out of the water and flopped on the floor boards to drain. Glancing up from these labours Carrol discovered the ship's lantern only a blur in the mist.

"Hallo! we've drifted," said he.

"And so we have," said the stoker agreeably.

"Hadn't we better try and get back?"

"Tryin' is all the gettin' back you'll do in a boat

without oars. We're better off where we are. If the old girl goes down we've a nice chance of not goin' down with her."

"I suppose they'll pick us up," suggested Carrol.

"Of course they will, if they have the sense to think of it. Will you have a drink?"

With that he unexpectedly produced a bottle from his singlet and handed it to Carrol, who took it gratefully, aware still of the sour taste of fear. He took a pull and gulped again, for it was brandy neat.

"Drink hearty," said the stoker, "I have another in me pocket. 'Twas by luck I reached into the bar in passin'."

"Thanks," said Carrol, handing it back. "One's enough as a reviver; I like it watered as a beverage."

"Never say so," said the stoker, taking a hearty swig with out discomposure. "I'm forgettin' me manners," he added, turning to the girl. "It's like you'll take a nip yourself, Miss?"

The politeness was ignored. The girl had remained this while seated at the stern, a patch of white swaying gently with the swell. She spoke now in a voice sharp with impatience.

"Why don't you call out and make them take us back?"

Carrol sent an experimental shout at what seemed to be a dim hint of light across the water. The other passenger started up to join him, and together they continued shouting with a forlorn effect into the mist.

The stoker lolled at his ease and made no offer to assist with noise.

"Can you hear them?" was all he said, complacently.

They could not. By the stress of listening, silence closed down on them, broken only by the plucking of water under the boat.

"I don't like this," said Carrol, and shouted again as at an unseen enemy. The other shouted too, in a voice that thinned to a bleat. No sound came back to them. Each listening pause intensified their isolation, lost in an empty space of ocean.

Carrol sat down viciously, throwing confidence to the devil. Like all self-inquisitive minds, he was aware of destiny as a personal malignant. The girl made an impatient sound, between anger and fear, and the other passenger turned hastily towards her.

"I hardly think there is cause for alarm," he said. "They'll surely miss us and wait to pick us up in the morning."

"It's more than you deserve if they do," said the stoker candidly. "You that is at the bottom of the trouble crowdin' in among the wimmen and knockin' me overboard. If you had your rights it's puttin' you in the water I'd be instead of pullin' you out of it."

"I was pushed—I had no such intention—I——"

He sat down, seeming to agitate an appeal for restored self-respect, which the stoker failed to endorse.

"Crowdin' in among the wimmen is all the parsons is good for," he said informatively. "Will you have a drink?" This with an offer of the bottle, which the other refused by a hasty gesture.

"You will not," said the stoker with satisfaction. "Sure I knew you wouldn't. You haven't the heart for it. Will I ever forget the bull-headed run you give at me over yonder. The luck of your life it was, missin' the punch I let out at you."

"I swear to you that I had no such intention. I was pushed."

"What does it matter how we got here?" said Carrol impatiently. "I was on the lower deck and jumped into the boat when that crowd started yelling again. An act of pure funk, and serve me dam' well right for making it."

"I am persuaded we will be picked up in the morning —persuaded of it," said the third passenger.

"You're easy persuaded and that's a fact," said the stoker.

His tone of derision stirred the girl to protective anger.

"Of course they'll wait to pick us up!" she exclaimed. "Absurd, thinking of anything else. They wouldn't dare go away and leave us and bad enough at that sitting up in a rotten boat all night."

Perched in the stern in her flimsy dance frock, she appeared to emanate opinion on three male idiots for her position there. Carrol and the other said nothing, depressed by their own alarms, but the stoker patronized her with a little gentlemanly consolation.

"Don't put yourself in a lather now, for a bit of a

lark will give you an appetite for breakfast, and you
with the laugh on them all for thinkin' you was at
the bottom of the ocean. For a night of it, I wish
I'd had the brains to grab more than two bottles. In
a bit of an upset of this sort I have a standin' rule to
give the bar a look-in at the first go-by. It's more
than one or two good booze-ups I've had by remem-
berin' that rule. But I was born in luck and that was
in Bull Lane, Dublin. You'd say I was the luckiest
man alive to hear the things I could tell about meself."

"Glad to hear it; I'm not lucky," said Carrol sourly.

"Then here's my luck agen yours an' that's luck for
both of us," said the stoker, taking a pull at his bottle.

That was how the newspapers a few days later came
to record as missing from the list of passengers landed
at Honolulu the names of Miss Sadie Patch, the Rev.
Fletcher Gibble, James Carrol, and Patrick Plunket,
stoker. . . .

CHAPTER TWO

I N THE dawn of their third day adrift the castaways came to an island. As yet, that was only a
feathery drift of cloud on the sea rim, lost in the
pallor of another day of fear. Its slow dawn turned
the dark sea grey, and showed their four bodies
stretched on the boat's floor boards, cramping sleep
with postures of discomfort.

That was the worst ingredient of their seafaring; a
cushion or two would have done much to mitigate
its prime motive of funk. They had biscuits and water
from the regulation supply in the boat. Heat they
had endured, but it was endurable. Nature had kept

17

decent manners with light winds and placid waters. They had drifted passively in a martyrdom of sore backsides by sitting all day on hard boards.

Carrol was the first to wake. He was the worst equipped for this adventure, having the best intelligence to forecast its possible disasters, which of course greatly magnified his sense of its present ill ease.

He rolled over on his face, glared vacantly, groaned consciously, and crawled to a seat with the strained expression of a rheumatic subject easing out his joints with caution.

There, to an interval of genuine depression he wilfully added depression; an act of propitiation to unknown malice.

His glum mask confessed him the dupe of a theory of happiness; its lines were hard angled, its nose long, its eyes sardonic and the corners of its lips depressed. Now with his black hair disordered and three days' stubble on his chin and his slack figure dressed in dirty white linen he gave malice a fair return for playing a rotten trick like this on him.

His glance rested on the three sleepers but ignored their complicity in his lot. All despairs of the body are reserved for us alone. Gibble the parson had given Sadie Patch his coat to lie on, and sprawled there in his black vest and trousers and his absurd clerical collar and his face presenting an expression of pained vacuity to the sky. He was a tall man with a small man's face. It defied identification in trenchant terms, beyond a general pinkiness. His hair was light, his eyes were

light; an irresponsible blood pressure bestowed on him
the infirmity of blushing; when he compressed his lips
little white dints appeared at the corners.

He lay midway in the boat, between Carrol and the
stoker in the stern and the girl in the bows. Like
the others she was stretched flat on her back, and the
night damps had moulded her skimpy frock to the
pattern of her rounded legs and the strong arch of
her body supporting two undaunted breasts. Sleep
accented the normal discontent of her heavy eyelids
and her lips were compressed to a pout. She breathed
with primitive ease through wide clean-cut nostrils.

But Carrol's glance failed to distinguish her as a girl
in that lonely boat; dry land and tobacco were realities
of desire and sex a trivial fantasy. Automatically his
pipe went to his mouth and he searched his pockets
for a shred of the divine narcotic. He did that at intervals all day long to exasperate defeated hopes. The
stoker had generously shared a plug of Navy Twist
with him, but that was long gone.

Carrol stared morosely at the brawny figure with the
black pipe clenched in its teeth; a creature immune from
discomfort or fatigue. His muscles padded him buoy-
antly up on the floor boards, the rise and fall of a
splendid chest pumped energy into a mechanism at ease
with life. In Carrol's glance at him was the envy of
the intellectual who sees the finest bodies squandered
on the crude denizens of earth.

Perhaps they deserve them, after all. Down one
side of the stoker's face was a jagged scar; two white

patches on his close-cropped skull marked other old wounds; the scornful heritage of a debauch of strength. His lips were firmly clamped under his stubbly moustache with an effect of derision, his nose had been broken and bettered thereby in form, and round his eyes were little wrinkles of blackguard good humour. He was a man of fifty with the vitality of youth intact. Promise of long life lay there or death by violence. . . .

Carrol glanced away with a frown; he was sick of conjuring images of finality in that boat. He reached over to wake Gibble, but arrested the mean impulse to rob him of sleep's releases. Perhaps the impulse did so. Gibble woke suddenly, his mouth agape and his eyes vacant with alarm. They rested on Carrol and were charged at once with uneasy remembrance.

"Another day," said Carrol glumly.

Gibble nodded, and turned to the great ball of the sun just lifting from the ocean. It awoke Sadie and the stoker, and petulance and mockery greeted the dawn.

"I'm soaked to the skin," complained Sadie.

"An' I'm dried to the bone," said Pat. "If I'd known we was goin' boatin' like this I'd have had every bottle was in the bar."

This might have been heroic but for its idiom of habit.

"I've lost another hairpin," said Sadie, searching irritably for it. This might have been more heroic still, but for its imbecility. To Carrol's scepticism it

was a fatuous invitation to destiny's perverted sense
of humour.

"I suppose we still eat," he said to Gibble.

Gibble unscrewed one of the patent tins under the
thwarts and doled out four allowances of biscuit. When
these were eaten he would hand out four half pan-
nikins of water. The job of administering their food
supply had been left to him because he had the optimism to calculate how long it would last on a fixed
allowance. He was very secret over this responsibility,
taking out only the proscribed quantity and sitting most
of the day with his back against the store, as if to protect
it from a combined assault.

But Sadie delayed the meal a moment.

"I wish you'd kindly turn your backs," she said
austerely.

All with docility gazed vacantly over the stern till
a flourish of skirts gave them the freedom of the boat
again.

Necessity vastly simplified the exercise of a secret
ritual. Carrol and Pat, without troubling Sadie to turn
her back on them, merely turned their backs on her.
Gibble alone waited for night to cover relief from the
pangs of a conscience burdened bladder. By the exercise of other repressions he was able to enforce martyrdom on it as with gritted teeth he silently endured.

They munched now, preoccupied over the intolerable
significance of food. When that was done each sought
a change of position to ease posteriors surfeited by hard
seats. Fear, the vulgar constituent of earth, made a

joke of heroics by its piddling allowance of petty annoyance. The record of their voyaging was in a tone of
complaint and a looking about for ships, unless all
succumbed to interludes of dozing. The stoker alone
talked, by an idiosyncratic demand for diversion. He
had the submerged literary faculty of the illiterate
which must talk and which can talk. He had also
the comedian's consciousness of entertaining and the
trained tale teller's trick of using any instance to intro-
duce a reminiscence. He did it with an air of gusto,
too, as if they were all seated comfortably in a pub
parlour.

". . . This sittin' about in boats is no more than
bein' in jail without a blanket, and if you'll mark my
opinion, there's mighty little difference bein' in one
place or the other if you happen to be cut off from
booze or a bit of fun with the girls. I've been in jails
of all sorts from Glasgow to Tampico in the Gulf of
Mexico, for what is bein' run in but findin' out you
can't bear the sight or smell of a policeman? The worst
eye in a human head is a policeman's, as them that
knows will bear me out. Bad bastards, the lot of them.
Have you ever seen them manhandle a feller once they
has him in a cell? I have, havin' been the feller was
manhandled. There was a Sydney cop I mind had me
marked for a bit of a friendly rough-up one night in
Lower George Street, and I give him all the trouble
he is askin' for before him and his mate has me run
in. I'll give him that much in for temper, but with
me handcuffed in the cell he fair kicked hell out of

me, an' got me a week on top of it for resistin' the
police. But wait now, and listen, while I tell you what
me and a lad named Ginger Conklin done to that cop
the night we has him alone behind Darling Harbour
wharves . . ."

No one really listened, though all were grateful for
a convention of the commonplace behind this indomitable flow of words.

But this morning even Pat was morose. He seemed to cast about the empty ocean for subject matter but gave it up. "I've a mind hell will be a dull hole too," he said, and spread himself out on the floor boards to drowse time away.

And all that while they drifted steadily down on the island. The current set with the swell, but moving as a part of the sea they had no sense of movement. Without their knowledge that smudge on the sea rim turned from grey to violet, from violet to gold, from gold to green, and all the while they sat glumly there as if disdaining this freak of escape from the sea.

It was Gibble who first found himself blinking at a marvel across the monotony of waves; a film pattern of earth on the skyline. He scrambled up with a startled cry, pointing, speechless. The others stared at him and at the sea, and all saw the island together.

"Land!" yelled Carrol, leaping up.

"Land!" gasped Gibble. He fell over a seat to point it out to Sadie.

"Land it is," said Pat.

"I call it providential," said Gibble. Even Carrol felt inclined to call it that.

"I call it a bit of an old island," said Pat. But his shoulders were squared, his pose was again jaunty; he assumed to disparage optimism because it was assured.

Fatigue had vanished from all. They could not sit still, but moved incessantly about the boat, trying to get a better view of the island. Sadie did her hair

twice, running swift fingers over her dress and smoothing out creases. She was preparing for civilized inspection. The others kept trying to calculate the boat's
speed and direction, which seemed to edge them west-
ward of the land. With the boat's hatchets they prized
up a couple of floor boards and were able to help the
boat's nose towards the land.

"We'll do it," said Carrol, forgetting his propitia-
tions of destiny's malice.

"Be sure we will, and have the bottom bumped out
of her on that bit of old rock," said Pat.

"Be damned; I can see a clear beach even from
here."

"What you cannot see is the rocks stickin' up all
round it, the such of which is called a reef."

This was treated as captiousness; nothing could be
simpler than their descent on that shining line of beach.
But a slow enough job it was getting there. By afternoon they were able to make out its tree shapes; palms
and banyans above a packed mass of undergrowth, and
last of all, a white line of foam that marked the reef.

Carrol and Gibble fidgeted about, trying to find an
opening to steer for. Sadie kept craning her neck for
houses. Pat lolled in the stern, diverted by all
possibilities.

"Sit down and take your duckin' in comfort," he
told the others, adding to Sadie, "Can you swim, then?"

"Of course I can," said Sadie impatiently.

"Then it's more than I can, so you'd better lend me
the tail of your shirt to pull me out of it."

Now they were close in and could watch the swell
break gently in patterns of foam at the hidden reef.
It was high tide and there was little surf, but once
caught in the backwash, they were aware of irresponsible forces that took charge of the boat in a frolic.
Floor boards were helpless to keep her head-on to the

reef. She blundered in sideways, hit a returning wave
and drenched them with spray. With that Sadie was
out of her one piece dress in two wriggles and out of
her petticoat in one more.

"You don't catch me getting tangled up in a silly
bit of surf like that," she said firmly, rolling her clothes
into a compact handful. Only Pat was gentleman

enough to admire the gallantry of her appearance in silk pants and a chemisette. "You have sense and as fine a figure as ever I see," said he, while Carrol and Gibble wrought madly with their floor boards.

Another wave tilted the boat's stem up and drove her swiftly forward, another slapped her back and came freely aboard. Flat rocks appeared and vanished in swirls of foam; a violent thump sent Carrol on his back in the half-submerged boat. "We're sinking," yelled Gibble.

They were, but on the other side of the reef. Pat put a leg over and found foothold on it. "Give me your hand then," he said to Sadie, and helped her down beside him. The others followed, knee-deep in the water. The reef was broad and flat enough, and all waded for the shore, with one mishap to Pat's account, by a slip and a ducking. Flat tide rocks made a causeway to the beach, to which they stumbled, swaying from the long motion of the sea, and dazed by a swift release from fear.

"We're here," said Carrol, astonished.

All stared about them, and at each other, and back at the silent white beach, shot with long afternoon shadows from the massed foliage behind it. Sea birds only, wheeling and dipping at the reef, broke its submerged calm.

"Dashed if I believe there's anyone here at all," said Carrol.

"Me either," said Pat.

Sadie at once got into her dress with a resolute air

that proposed putting a stop to rot of that sort at once.

"Absurd," she said.   "There simply *must* be people here."

Standing there in her slim evening shoes and frock an imperative was understood, and no one had the courage to question its rationality.   They moved along the beach, staring irresolutely at its packed undergrowth, which was like a moulded wall of green.

"There's another beach beyond the headland; I noticed it from the boat," said Gibble.

By the flat tide rocks they turned the headland and opened up a smaller beach, banked like the other with dark undergrowth.   In the shadows of afternoon its desolation was manifest.

"I wish we'd had the sense to pocket a few biscuits," said Carrol, and all were aware of hunger.

"Oh, well, no use standing about here.   Let us try inland," said Gibble.

He pushed into the undergrowth, the others straggling after him without inspiration.   It was dementedly tangled, very hot, and Sadie was in trouble with her flimsy skirt at every twist.

"But this is impossible," she cried, showing a rent in its sacred fabric with dismay.

"Hadn't you better stay on the beach?   We'll see what's to be seen and come back for you," suggested Carrol.

"Well, don't be long, for heaven's sake."

They were not overlong in that scrub.   Half an hour's worming about its tangle assured them that no primitive earth is designed for man. Shut off from the sea air, its soggy heat drenched them in sweat and melted energy from a meagre diet of biscuits and water. Only Gibble's panting insistence of "We really must find fruit" kept them struggling on.

"God in hell, there's no standing this," exclaimed Carrol at last.

"And no fruit but thorns to be got either," said Pat, picking one from his arm.

Gibble swabbed a face the colour of beetroot, already sun-peeled by exposure in the boat.

"It strikes me! Those palms near the beach——"

"Of course, coconuts!" said Pat, enlightened. "I ought to have me head read, that has seen them growin' in the West Indies."

At the first palm an oversight was confirmed with immense relief to all, peering aloft into its tufted shadow.

"Coconuts, sure an' all," said Pat, taking a grip of the tree with arms and legs. The climb taxed his endurance but he reached the fruit and threw down a supply which was gathered in Gibble's coat and lugged back to the beach, where Sadie had made a resthouse of a flowering hibiscus and there awaited them.

"Did you find anyone?" she called.

"Coconuts!" called Gibble.

That disposed of other matters while they sat about at ease and guzzled the fruit, which said delicious things to their parched bellies. "Glorious," said Carrol at intervals, "Providential," endorsed Gibble. . . .

A latent fear was disposed of too; they were assured of food. It confirmed the right to release their tired joints and wallow with full bellies on the warm sand; it lifted the cursed stress of thinking. Even Sadie confessed the moment relieved of all needs save the need for rest. Gibble spread his coat for her on the sand and with one long relaxing sigh she was asleep.

"The wench has sense," said Pat, and turned over where he lay. Carrol tried to think of precautions over their position on an open beach, with an unknown earth behind them and the long rays of the sun already purpling the sea, but tiredness ached through his joints. With warm sand beneath him and green leaves above, he dropped fathoms deep into the security of sleep.

Gibble sat on, seeming to wait till each was soundly unconscious, as if he had a matter on his mind which required indulgence in private. With a furtive air, he now went a little apart and offered up a prayer of thanksgiving to the kind God who had bumped them adrift in an open boat, subjected them to unrelenting terrors, and lobbed them ashore on a desolate island to a diet of coconuts and a future as vacant as the distant sea rim.

CHAPTER THREE

CARROL woke in a flurry of alarm and a sensation of being taken apart at the joints. At the first movement a contraction of the sinews shot his knees up to his chin, and gasping like a fish he tried to rub sense back to his miserable members. His breathless curses brought Gibble blinking back to consciousness and he, seeking to arise, let out a yelp that woke Sadie and Pat.

"Is it bitten you are?" asked Pat, for Gibble was grappling at his person with a face of mortal anguish.

"It's—phew!—got me in the—phew—back," gasped Gibble.

He crawled feebly to a tree and there erecting himself, took a brief jaunt across the sand in the doubled up posture of those pill advertisements of people with pains in the back.

"He has a list to starboard, the queer feller," said Pat dispassionately.

Gibble shambled back and greeted Sadie with the wan smile of suffering heroism.

"I hope you slept well," he said feebly.

"Slept well!" Sadie brought a glazed glare to bear on this perverted inquiry. "I hope I never live to pass such a horrible vile, beastly, rotten, damnable night again."

"You've defined it," groaned Carrol, gingerly restoring his legs to normal length.

"It's the sand, you know," confessed Gibble. "It packs under you and the cold strikes upward . . ."

They sat forlornly in a row, watching the sea slowly gather the pale light of dawn, till the sun hove a rim over the horizon and shot a glittering pathway to the island. It restored them to partial animation, though Carrol failed to express appreciation of coconuts as a breakfast food. "Bacon and eggs," he said, with a gastric scowl at his coconut.

"For the love of God don't speak of it; I was this minute thinkin' of steak and onions," said Pat.

Gibble had turned his kidneys to the sun and optimism was a little revived in him. "It was thoughtless of us sleeping on sand like that; tonight we must make a better arrangement," he said.

"You don't imagine we're going to spend another night *here*, do you?" demanded Sadie indignantly.

"Well—no. That is—no," said Gibble, funking controversy on that point.

"I should think *not*. It's obviously quite a big place

and there must be people on it. You two"—she nodded at Carrol and Pat—"can go and find them. Mr. Gibble can stay here with me. I don't like being left alone—not *here*, anyway. And I must have some sort of a change of clothes, no matter what."

This was fanaticism, but the others submitted to it.

"As well walkin' as sittin'," said Pat, getting up. Carrol joined him after a moment's vacillation.

"All the same, you'd better get something fixed up against tonight," he said to Gibble.

Gibble nodded, watching the pair slouch off across the sand to the headland and disappear beyond it.

"I have a feeling that they will be successful, quite," said Gibble, who felt nothing of the sort.

Sadie nodded briefly and wound her wristlet watch. She had done that every morning on the boat. Rationality refused to countenance absurd intrusions on its ritual. She now took out her hairpins and put them carefully aside while she shook out her hair. It was very long, the colour of raw sienna, and flicked with bronze in the high lights. She had refused to scarify this wealth to the modern crop, but did her best to keep fashion in countenance by screwing it into flat coils over each ear. Thus hairpins were an afflicted necessity to her. Now with her hair loosened and tossed about her shoulders the sullen lines of her face were softened and she looked a handsome creature. Gibble thought so, in this bizarre experience of a girl's morning toilet, watching her while she combed it with her fingers, soothed by the warmth and the gravity of her occupation.

"I shall have to plait it," she said at last. "Without a comb, what else can I do?"

"You are wise, very wise," said Gibble with fervour. He moved closer, with an inspired eye on the hairpins. "Hadn't I better put these in my pocket for you? They may get lost in the sand."

"Thanks," said Sadie.

"Fish-hooks," said Gibble, in an aside to that kind God of his. He edged away and was presently busy in the scrub, lugging up armfuls of bracken and pulling down branches. It was hot work, to be endured with a fine sense of male resourcefulness. As the sun rose it was hotter still, and harder to endure with the creaming of the surf out there offering a delicious refreshment.

"I'm going for a swim," called Sadie from the beach.

"Splendid," encouraged Gibble, producing a face of mottled scarlet from the scrub. "Don't bother about me; I shall be in here most of the day."

"That's all right, I'll try the little beach; it shelves better."

She went off, leaving Gibble to sweat and itch under an inhibition against uncovering his carcass where a woman might see it. In sight of glittering water too. Still, with Sadie out of the way he was able to select a site for the camp, and there began stripping boughs and twigs to erect a series of bird's nest couches; sweating sacrificially to the benediction of Sadie's head bobbing in the surf out there, and the silver flash of her body as it turned in the water. He was very careful not to look that way. . . .

Carrol and Pat did not return till late in the afternoon, and they arrived unexpectedly from the other end of the beach, plodding wearily into a partial regeneration of last night's discomforts. Gibble had laid out boughs criss-crossed with twigs and piled with feathery growths. Over one of these he had built a shelter of boughs, and under it Sadie was seated with her hair neatly plaited, and an air of languorous refreshment about her as the effect of having spent most of the day in the water. Gibble had flopped on the sand beside her, grimed with sweat and dirt and gaping after his labours.

"What luck?" he hailed the wayfarers, aware of none by their dispirited advance.

Carrol only threw himself on the nearest pile with a groan of fatigue. Pat paused to empty his singlet and pockets of a quantity of small round fruits. He then delivered compactly the spoil of a topographical survey.

" 'Tis an island three miles square, or round, as you will have it. By the trouble of walkin' it, 'tis a hundred. There's nothin' on it but flies and saygulls."

"You must be mad," cried Sadie in alarm.

"I am, with trampin' the soles off me feet," he sat down to pull off his boots and examine a blistered heel.

Sadie was now staring her widest. She had two special facets of emotion and two faces for recording them. When she was undisturbed, or contented, or merely not thinking, her eyelids drooped and her lips compressed to a pout; she looked ill-tempered. If anger or interest or excitement intruded on this detachment, her eyebrows shot up into two brilliant curves, her eyes opened wide and stayed open, and she was gifted with instant volubility if not coherence.

"I tell you the thing's impossible. Look at my dress; it won't last a week. And my shoes; one of them's burst already. And no underwear! One pair of pants a petticoat a chemise worn for nearly a week. I had four boxes on the *Minorca*, four, not counting what I bought in San Francisco, the prizes were wonderful though I never could count dollars, impossible to resist them and I will *not* wear soiled underlinen and everybody knows what ship's washing is even if you tip the steward and now with rags falling off me I shall go mad."

"It's on the beach you are and no mistake," said Pat candidly.

"But I tell you the thing's simply impossible."

No one denied it.

"Impossible," stamped Sadie, enraged at their apathy.

"Yes, impossible," said Carrol, rousing himself to kick off his shoes. "But life's impossible, if it comes to that, and we go on living it. I suppose we'll go on doing it here as usual."

"As usual! You call it usual, sitting about all day looking at that rotten sea and eating coconuts," stormed Sadie.

"Don't put yourself in a lather now," soothed Pat. "In a week's time you'll think it was what you was made for."

A week's time! ! ! Sadie was quite unable to bear an unmentionable hypothesis. She plumped down on her bird's nest and kicked up two frantic heels. From that she recovered to turn on Gibble an air of imperious command.

"Mr. Gibble, you'll simply *have* to do something."

"Certainly—of course," agreed Gibble in haste. "We shall—er—signal ships. There will be ships passing here frequently. We'll build a flagstaff and—er—signal to them."

An illusion of resource appeared to calm Sadie. She regained her other face, with a surprising effect of having mislaid it for the moment.

"I dare say we *could* stand a week of it, washing one's clothes while sun-baking, and I will say that's a perfect beach for swimming, though the reef spoils the surf at low tide."

"A swim," said Carrol, roused. "Why didn't I think of it before? Come on, before the sun goes off the water."

Gibble rose gladly; Pat followed, squaring his shoulders jauntily. "Cook us a coconut stew and put your little finger in to sweeten it," he said to Sadie as he went.

Sadie's eyelids refused jocularity either on that subject or from that source. She had borrowed Gibble's penknife to trim her nails, and went on doing so, using the kid top of her shoe to polish them. Three male heads appearing and disappearing beyond the headland and the sound of their voices exhilarated by refreshment carried a pleasant sense of security to the beach. Now that the sun was behind the island the air was temperate, and the sea for miles a flat panel of turquoise, broken at the reef by a languid curl of foam. Even a tragic deprivation of drapers' shops receded in the well-being of that placid interlude.

All admitted it, gathered for the evening meal of fruit. Gibble's couches were really a luxury after the long conflict of their bones with hard surfaces. Besides, Gibble had found a little stream of fresh water close to the camp and had filled several gouged out coconut shells with it, and the new fruit brought back by Pat relieved a dominant flavour of coconut.

"They are guavas, I think," said Gibble, sampling one. "We had some at Honolulu, but I doubt these are quite ripe."

"They're eatable; that's the only present respect I'd pay to any substance on earth," said Carrol.

"Certainly, certainly, they are a delicious fruit, when ripe. These will be, in a week or so. I foresee great advantages from this discovery. There must be other fruit here—bread fruit, for example."

"Which I suspect sounds like bread and tastes like potatoes," said Carrol.

"What's wrong with potatoes, anyhow; roasted in their jackets with a dash of pepper and salt, begob!" said Pat.

"Lobster mayonnaise," said Sadie, closing her eyes to shut out a *too* sweet vision.

They went on calling over foods as a perverse source of appetite for a lack of them. Gibble appeared to discover an uneasy speculation on this subject, and kept glancing at Carrol and Pat as if about to ask them something which he failed to ask. When Carrol stretched himself at last on his brushwood couch he gave a sigh which admitted, yet craved repletion.

"These doss-heaps of yours are good," he said to Gibble. "I would find them the last thing in Roman luxury if I had something to smoke."

"I've got some cigarettes, if they'll do," said Sadie.

"What!" yelled Carrol, leaping up.

"Funny, I forgot till this moment that I had them."

Sadie wore at her waist a slim gold chain to which was attached a ring of box keys, a fan, and a flat gold cigarette case. This she detached and tossed to Carrol, whose clutch revealed its contents to be seven cigarettes. Down on his knees he went and reverently kissed Sadie's shoe.

"Divine adorable and only perfect girl on earth," he said.

"Pooh!" said Sadie, not displeased to find herself so handsomely substituted as an image of tobacco.

"Three and a half each," said Carrol to Pat.

"Damn the odd one, keep it yourself."

"Generous whole-hearted fellow, I will. I would rob my dying father of his last smoke on earth."

He divided the cigarettes, put one in his mouth and the case in his pocket, "I'll keep it till they're smoked," he said to Sadie, and pulled out a box of matches. It brought with it a pocket comb which fell on the sand, and that was Sadie's turn to discover that the earth still had priceless gifts to bestow.

"A comb!" she cried, snatching it up.

"Keep it; I forgot till this moment that hair has its uses."

He struck a match, which did not ignite; another, which also failed. Gibble was peering at each experiment, and uttered a sound of consternation.

"They're damp," said Carrol in alarm. He struck one now with infinite precaution but without result. All were useless; they had been wet in the ducking at the reef. Carrol slumped down and gazed dumbly at his cigarette; a symbol of destiny's ingenuity in frustrating hope.

"Awful," said Gibble. "I feared this. That's why I dared not ask if we had any matches."

He joined Carrol in a pose of collapse.

"Wait now," said Pat. "We're not beaten yet. Have a look at the inside of that."

He tossed Gibble a brass match box with a tightly fitted lid. Gibble clicked it gingerly open and took out a wax vesta. For a moment he feared to test it, gazing with awe from face to face. But the test was made and the match flared finely in the dusk and Carrol uttered a cry of thanksgiving as he leaned forward to light his cigarette, followed by Pat.

Gibble counted the matches carefully, restored to confidential relations with his kind God.

"Twenty-four," he said. "These must be put away in a place where no damp can reach them. And once our fire has been lighted it must never be allowed out. We must keep it going on a careful system."

In the dusk it could be seen that Sadie had resumed her staring face.

"You talk as if we were going to stay here for *ever*," she said.

"Only till we signal a ship," said Gibble hurriedly.

The others said nothing.

CHAPTER FOUR

GIBBLE had foreseen the advantage of guavas to a diet of coconuts; what he did not foresee was the collective bellyache that arrived as the effect of eating them in an unripe state.

It seemed that the dawn must again witness their most urgent despairs. They were all up in it, darting for the scrub, griped at unmercifully and convinced of destructive essences at work on them.

A pallid group the sun came up to look at, contorted on their funeral pyres of brushwood and gazing fearfully at each other for symptoms of disaster.

"It's poison, I'm convinced," wailed Sadie.

"It's worse than that," said Pat. "No poison would be equal to the bellygruntin' I have this minute."

"Poison would be a relief to this; it's a new disease invented on islands," groaned Carrol.

"No—no! it's—it's those guavas," quavered Gibble, restraining himself nobly in Sadie's presence. But he had within him forces more potent than all the inhibitions of Christendom, and ran suddenly into the scrub with the hunted expression of one who must outrace a monstrous calamity. And, in short, Gibble lost that race. . . .

When he came out of the scrub later it was some distance from the camp and he walked with a peculiar straddling motion, as if he had leg irons on. By the flat rocks he vanished round the headland.

"He's gone to drown himself, the queer feller," said Pat languidly.

No one bothered to question a rationality like that. Reservations had ceased to exist for them; appearance was discarded. Pat was no more than a pair of large feet sticking out of a pile of brushwood and at intervals they kicked spasmodically. Carrol was a contortion and a mop of hair from which groans issued. Sadie's convulsions tied her legs into knots and caused her in special extremities to beat her skull on the earth with fainting outcries. They were suspended in an awful incuriosity to all things save the potency of an unripe guava. When its gripings were at last defeated, postures of defeat alone survived that trenchant battle.

They lay thus all the morning and no one spoke of food. When Gibble came slinking back with a muttered reference to an early walk their cultured debility did not distinguish a private disaster on his part from the common lot.

But it did them good, that gastric visitation. It restored them to a world made perfect by a release from the gripes. As a natural evacuant it left them with a ravening hunger which finely inaugurated their first capture of crabs.

These fantastic edibles were discovered at evening

scuttling about the beach and in no time a supply was disabled and coerced into a bundle made by Gibble's coat. They went quite mad over that event, the hunters galloping about between crabs and water and Sadie screaming and skipping and pointing out the large ones.

"They'll be delicious, roasted on the coals," she said, gloating lewdly over the crustaceous bundle.

Lumps of coral were carried up to make a cooking place and on it the fire was sacrificially laid by Gibble. A solemn moment when the flame ran crackling through the kindling twigs, and all were forced to an excessive secretion of saliva while waiting for coals to mature that crabs might be roasted, and roasted they were in spite of some formal objections from the crabs, but that was a trifle well rewarded by the handsome things said about crabs round that camp fire.

They gathered wood and kept it going, and it vastly enlivened the night. Gibble tended it with fanatic zeal; Carrol smoked another cigarette. Pat had used up his the night before, lighting one from the other with a prodigal contempt for a meagre pleasure. Still, he reclined expansively and found the event excellent. For the first time in their seafaring, all were aware of a social relaxation. . . .

Sadie sat contentedly fiddling with a bracelet, her discontented eyelids drooped reposefully over the palliative of cooked food, and the firelight flickering up her long plaits and bare arms.

"It suits you doing your hair like that," said Carrol. "Only a girl with your build could carry off plaits with dignity. All you want is a chaplet of thin gold and you'll be a Norwegian princess—'Brunnhilde at the Funeral Pyre.'"

"The very thing I was this minute thinkin'," said Pat. "It's like a queen she is, sittin' there with bracelets on her arms."

Gibble, in search of a compliment, was forced to

borrow from Carrol. "Yes, undoubtedly, you should always wear your hair like that," he said solemnly.

This was very right and proper, and Sadie accepted it frankly as beauty's tribute, a little overdue, perhaps.

"I never would cut it in spite of everyone nagging at me but I've got such a frightful lot of it that there's no doing it up really flat. All the same with my height I will not wear a bob."

"You are not only beautiful but very wise," said Carrol.

Sadie preened a queenly neck and swept an approving glance downward at herself. With equal candour, the others approved of her too. The mysterious rarity of a woman was revealed to them.

Gibble found himself strangely moved. Incomplete formulas announcing felicity of being were pressed on him. That kind God was hovering about just outside the range of firelight, a little hurt because no one invited him to join the circle.

"You must admit we've been wonderfully blessed," he said suddenly.

An intonation invented in pulpits alarmed Carrol; there was a dangerous shining of exaltation in Gibble's eye.

"Wonderfully blessed," he repeated, with a gesture that included Sadie, the fire and a heap of crab shells. "Just think of what might have happened to us in that boat! And here we are, safe, provided with food, fire, a—er—splendid climate. We must acknowledge a guiding hand here; a hand of vast benevolence."

"Benevolence?" said Carrol cautiously. "I'll admit an ingenious exercise of dramatic contrasts, but benevolence—well——"

"Come," encouraged Gibble, "consider how only this morning—" He ruled out that instance of unblessedness hurriedly. "Consider at least how quickly we are restored to health."

"Well, you can't call a system that gives you a frenzied bellyache as a stimulus to enjoying a feed of crabs exactly benevolent. You wouldn't call a ruffian who knocked you down benevolent for picking you up again."

"But, one moment. These contrasts in adversity are designed to test the spirit of our acceptance of them."

"Yes, I believe that is the theory. But it overlooks the system that devised the tests, which is obviously malevolent to the last degree."

"Impossible! We could not exist under such a system."

"Of course, we couldn't. We don't, either. We live under a fatuous theory of optimism in order *not* to find out what the system is doing to us."

Gibble blinked rapidly, scrambling among the defences of that notorious optimism.

"But, you speak as if life were a positive evil."

"Life! I'm not talking about life, but the system by which we experience it, and that's a stinking mean lousy process of frustration and nothing else. Oh, I know, we cling to it like blazes all the same. Apply Sam Johnson's test of clapping a pistol to my head and

I'll yell for help. But that's the trick that keeps us going on with the foolery; funk—pure funk."

"But—this is extreme. Adversity, yes. But there are compensations. Consider life's vast gifts to us."

"Rot, life gives us nothing. The only gifts we have are from men, and dam' few of those. I'll admit music; I couldn't live without music."

"No, no, I mean, how much happiness we have to compensate us for suffering."

"We have no such thing as happiness. We have just enough release from suffering to allow us to stand it. Of course, there are one or two things worth having; tobacco and girls and—yes, I'll admit one almost perfect ingredient—getting drunk with a cheerful group of idiots."

"There you have it," said Pat, enlivened by a rational remark. "Is not the feelin' grand to hit the face of a feller in friendliness and booze?"

"Grand," said Carrol. "At the same time I count a punch on the nose one of the most awful things that can happen. You'll have to decide, Gibble, whether the joy of punching a nose compensates for the anguish of having it punched."

"Tut! tut!" protested Gibble.

"Well, it's your theory of benevolent compensations. All the same, the balance is all on the side of malevolence. I'd forego the joy of punching fifty noses to save having my own punched once. So would you. I won't answer for Pat, but he's got a cast-iron nose."

"I have not. This bump I have on it was got by a

thump from a bottle in Liverpool, and put me in such a temper I come near killin' the feller that done it."

"Well, I call that fair compensation and almost justi-fies Gibble's theory of benevolence. But, of course, the eternal muddle on this problem is obvious enough. Life is a marvellous thing as an image while as a fact it is pure drivel. The best we can do is to extract a bit of fun out of the drivel. Booze and girls, that's all it amounts to. And we're deprived of them here; hanged if I can see what compensation your theory can offer in exchange for them."

"Oh, come, come, this is wild talk——"

"Sadie will bear me out; she's been cut off from a more passionate debauch than any of us. Drapers' shops, for example."

"Pooh!" objected Sadie. "I think it's just as fright-fully awful being cut off from everything. Not only parties; books. I read quite a lot. Give me a really good book and I simply can't put it down. And music. We're very musical at our place. I don't mean jazz, though, of course, we dance a lot, but classical music. Why, I never missed a single Italian opera last season."

"There you are," said Carrol to Gibble. "You've got to admit that even Italian opera has claims to com-pete with a benevolent feed of crabs."

"I cannot say that I am strongly moved to music myself," said Gibble solemnly.

"Still, jazz, drapers' shops and Elinor Glyn are a mouthful of deprivations for that theory of benevolence of yours to swallow. And besides, you haven't told us what it has especially deprived you of."

Gibble pondered. "Well, there's my work——" he began, but Carrol cut that short.

"I won't admit work. I preach in a tin Bethel myself——I mean, I make a living scribbling rot for newspapers. A degraded job which I'm dam' glad to be rid of. Where's your ingredient of debauch that Sadie and Pat and I have admitted?"

Gibble smiled weakly to say, "I see you are joking," and pulled his face back to the correct elongation for pulpit topics.

"I am not bigoted, far from it. In fact, my views have been held to be too broad. Amusement, harmless amusement, I believe to have its place. At our parish hall I have encouraged church aid dances. It is permissible to relieve the stress of life within certain limits. But that stress remains our spiritual stimulus. We are assured within ourselves that by its conquest we may hope to attain a——er——future state of happiness."

Carrol confessed defeat by the peculiar art of pulpits.

"That will be very nice," he said.

Pat turned over on his elbow to inspect Gibble. He appeared to think it time that a misuse of the true function of talk should be accounted for.

"I've no use for this religion at all," he told Gibble. "It's nothin' but a dread put on us by the priest. For causin' trouble I never seen the like of it. There was a lad by the name of Antonio Monigetti was stoker in the old *Monkseaton* had a picture of Jasus stuck up over his bunk, and was for ever offerin' to knife the lot of us for sayin' this Jasus was a dago in a nightshirt with a tin plate on his head."

Carrol fell over on his back to laugh; Gibble's expression was that of a man who has suddenly swallowed his false teeth.

"For a dago he was, this Jasus," said Pat didactically, "The proof which is these dagos has him spread-eagled in their churches burnin' stinks to him night and day. A nasty revengeful lot they are. I mind a bit of a dago priest we had in India by the name of Father Berlindin was regimental chaplain; a squib of a feller with a face the colour of a pig's belly and a long black beard on it."

"A Marist," suggested Carrol.

"Sure you've hit the very word; a Marist he was. There was others the like of him there, all with beards you could stuff a bed with. But for causin' trouble this Father Berlindin is the worst of the lot. I mind once he has been fastin' for weeks and his breakfast is cooked and waitin' for him on the table. But while he is preachin' at the holy Romans, and a sight of them there was in the old Quane's Own Royal Welsh Fusiliers, me and Rimmy Burke is eatin' his breakfast on him. He run to the Colonel to complain of us, but sure he had a down on us already for takin' the pledge on him."

"He encouraged booze, did he?"

"He did not; he hated the very smell of it. His standin' order is that anyone takin' the pledge would have two rupees and a cigar. So me and Rimmy Burke

not havin' the price of a drink on us, takes the pledge
on him.   The Colonel give us six days cells.   I mind
now this Father Berlindin's beard gettin' him into
trouble with a lad by the name of Paddy Cotter pullin'
a handful of it out one night he is lookin' over a fence
with it."

"Had Paddy taken the pledge on him too?"

"He had not.   He had a wench with him behind that
fence and that was his reasons for not bein' looked at.
And it's the livin' truth of God I'm tellin' you that
Paddy Cotter told the Colonel next mornin' that he
pulled the whiskers out of Father Berlindin for a love
token to be made into a horsehair watch chain."

Carrol laughed, enjoying the pose of comedian behind an Irishman's assumption of innocent candour.
He was aware of a literary diversion to be grateful
for.   Besides, it had nicely quelled pulpit indecencies
from Gibble. . . .

Sadie yawned, bored by this impersonal male gabble.
And as it continued to forget that talk was designed to
tell a woman interesting things about herself she took
herself off to bed and was asleep in five minutes.

Gibble found himself left alone.   He sat on the other
side of the fire and did not listen to Pat's talk.   That
was defensive, but his thoughts were bemused too.
Something had gone very wrong at a gathering especially called on for a little abasement to Gibble's kind
God.   He did not discover that the wrong thing about
their refusal to abase themselves to his God was that
they denied him an exercise of exaltation.   How is a

man to announce himself worthy save as the creature
of a worthy God? . . .

Carrol went on encouraging reminiscence from Pat,
who required no encouragement. He had the gift of
his race, a flow of facile speech. He had also that
charming national intonation which placates the ear at
the expense of the intellect. Only a species of tonal
mesmerism can account for the magnificent drivel
talked by Irish orators.

Gibble sat on, picking up little twigs to light them
at the fire and watch them burn out with a vacant eye.
Sometimes he cast a hasty glance behind him, either to
see if that kind God was still dodging about, or at the
dim line of foam at the reef that shut him out from
their island prison. . . .

Somewhere over that sea rim was the great safe
herd, all living alike, thinking alike, protected millions
deep from the danger of a single idea. A terrible earth
this would be, detached from the inertia of Faith and
tossed into the unknown space of lawless thoughts and
deeds . . .

Suddenly it became necessary not to think of these
things. He began to bustle about, collecting wood for
the fire and making it up to burn as slowly as possible.
He must impress on himself the habit of waking at
intervals to keep it going. With an effect of taking
cover he crawled into his doss-heap, leaving Pat and
Carrol talking.

CHAPTER FIVE

PAT had given Sadie a week's time to find herself at home on an island, but in a week's time he was as muddled as the rest of them to account for a mislaid system of life. It takes more than a week to regroup a fresh set of conventions, and merely looking about for food does not convince you of a stable existence.

They had plenty of food. By making lines from twisted fibres and hooks from Sadie's hairpins, barbed with a nail file in Carrol's knife, they caught fish in the lagoon and from the reef. It was a good employment and filled in a fair proportion of time. Time was their evil; they had too much of it. . . .

There was the fire to look after, which Gibble took on himself, though all helped to gather wood for it. There was fruit to search for. There were proposals to build a hut, but with nothing to cut timber with, that enterprise stopped at rude shelters over their sleeping lairs. There was swimming and there was talk. . . .

As deprivations to a theory of compensations already discussed, there were interludes when there was nothing to do, nowhere to go, nothing to talk about and no one to talk to.

These brought to the surface an idiosyncratic rebellion against the boredom of life.

Gibble found its best solution in making activity its own objective. He went about picking up shells when there was nothing else to do. He collected grasses and fibres and coconut shells and lumps of coral; anything that could be picked up in one place and carried to another. An illusion of utility sufficed him.

Pat was safe while he could talk, but all talk hovers over an abyss of non-existence, where to be detached from an audience is death. And when Carrol had enough of Pat's talk he cleared off into the scrub by himself. Like all who are aware of a dream of isolation, he supported depression best when alone.

Sadie was the one who brought rebellions to climax, because of those two faces of hers. Under her mask of discontented contentment she seemed to forget all about their bizarre situation. She did forget, because she had great powers of not thinking and a passion for salt water. One process involves the other. Sadie was a Sydney girl. Her home was at Coogee and she had grown up in the surf. The small beach was given up to her and she sun baked there for hours.

It might be guessed that her capacity for narcotism was a protective inertia, because when she came out of it the others had to endure an explosion of nerves. No terms were tragic enough to account for their awful lot; idiots were responsible for it.

There were excuses, to be sure. . . .

She came out of the scrub one morning to the camp, where Carrol and Gibble were sorting out fishing lines, Her eyebrows hoisted a danger signal and her eyes were darkly pigmented and she issued an imperious command without explaining it.

"One of you will have to give me a shirt."

"What, to wear?" asked Gibble.

"No, of course not." She stamped. "Kindly understand that I must have it, that's all."

"That's all right, take mine," said Carrol, pulling it off.

"Mind, I shall have to tear it."

"Of course."

She snatched the shirt and went off into the scrub with it, leaving Gibble staring after her.

"That's very curious," he said.

"Curious! Well, you can call it that, I suppose. I call it a blasted nuisance; you can't put your arm round a girl without being nagged at by its idiotic threat. It's like everything else in the system; a nemesis out of all proportion to its rewards. Think of all the gallant little imbeciles of girls who are wondering at this moment whether last night's embrace is going to be next month's maternity. I've had a few bad times over that question myself, barring the blessed resources of a little antiseptic surgery."

Gibble became suddenly active gathering up fishing tackle. His frown excluded Carrol and there were little white dents at the compression of his lips.

"I don't hold with that," he said at last. "Taking life—even the life of the embryo—is murder."

"That's the embryo's look out."

"One MUST—NOT—TAKE—LIFE!"

"Rot! How are you going to prove it's life? It might be only a human being."

Gibble went off fishing at once, leaving Carrol sneering at his retreating back.

"The things they mustn't have said to them," he muttered. "A code to keep life out of bounds. All the same, I'm a fool to talk to that goat; how the deuce can we expect them to face a process that can only expose them . . ."

He ruminated for an interval and arrived at a discovery.

"Hell! I never realized before how much of my

life has been made up of talk. It's obvious, with no one to talk to here."

By that road he discovered something else.

"No wonder I've never done any work."

He could face that confession on the island, since there was no possibility on the island of doing work. Like most intelligent young Australian frustrates, Carrol was always going to write a novel, or a play, or a book of essays, or something. . . .

Pat came along the beach from his special job of climbing for coconuts, and threw an armful down at the cooking place. With that he and Carrol stared detachedly at each other, at the beach and back at each other.

"Is it fishin' or is it swimmin'?" asked Pat at last.

"Swimming, I suppose."

They went down to the water and submerged a suspended existence for the time being. Carrol swam and dived and floated and exercised a diversion, while Pat lay in the shallows. He could not swim and refused to learn. "I've been too near drownin' to see the sense of it," he said. "A man is born to his proper end and I'll die on land with my boots on."

They came out to sprawl on the sand and take the reward of a consciously idle interlude. Gibble crouched at the end of the reef, intently fishing. It allowed him to arrive at a state of hypnotic abstraction to anything but a tug at his line. Sadie had drifted listlessly back to the camp and thrown herself on her pile of brushwood, where she lay without movement.

"She has the dumps on her this mornin', has Lady Sadie," remarked Pat.

"Yes, rotten for her, under any terms.   Worse than for us even at its best."

"How do you make that out?   Wouldn't I think meself in luck to be wrecked on an island with three wimmen an' me the only man among them?"

Carrol stared a moment at this outlook on their peculiar grouping, but let speculation on it lapse.

"How did you get that hole in your thigh, Pat?" he asked.

"A bullet done it, a soft-nosed bullet at that, fired by a bloody Boer at Bloemfontein."

"And that cut down the cheek?"

"A Burman give me that with a crooked knife they uses in them parts.   And this mark here"—he searched his scalp—"I come by in a bit of a scrap in Afghanistan. This one—now let me think.   Was it bein' hit with a fire shovel done that or was it the thump I got by a feller let down the chain slings on me at Vera Cruz? But the funniest things about me is the marks I haven't got, and what was that but fallin' into an empty hold as full as a tick and not a scrape on me.   Did you ever know a man has had such luck as me?"

"You call it luck, do you?"

"Wouldn't any one of them have killed another man?"

He expanded his chest, flexed his biceps, and gazed luxuriously over his indomitable limbs.

"Am I not the grandest figure of a man you ever looked at?" he said with honourable candour.

"You are.   I'd give the thing I call my intelligence for your body any day."

"You'd have the best of the bargain.   What is brains good for but to torment the guts out of yourself?   I mind a feller was in the old Quane's Own Royal Welsh Fusiliers could read Greek and Latin in cold print, and what does he do one night but put a bullet through the brains was such a nuisance to him."

"Sensible fellow."

"It's bowels I am, not brains.   There's Gibby yonder sittin' up like an old sea fowl I hope has a good catch for us.   I never seen meself so fond of food as I am in this place."

"Yes, it's the only dissipation left us.   I'll become a belly god with another month of this."

"It wouldn't be a bad life at all if an old wreck would only pile up on the reef there with a cargo of booze. Did I tell you how me an' the port watch wrecked a ship and come by a booze-up?   In the Gulf of Mexico it was; we was runnin' cargoes of fruit from Vera Cruz to New York in the old *Tingqua* an' the captain was part owner of her.   You'll bear them facts in mind.   The trouble come by three of our mates bein' run in at Vera Cruz.   In reason the captain could have paid their fines, but he ships three dagos instead and sails without them.   That put the lot of us agen him, port and starboard watches, an' we makes it up between us to give him no more than steam enough to bring his cargo in rotten.

"The starboard watch has first shift, and man to man they kept their word, and six or seven knots was all the engineers could get out of her. Then it was our turn, and I mind old McKinney the chief eyein' us over as we come down the engine-room ladders. 'Let's see what the Black Pan Watch can do,' sez he, 'for them Starboard hoodlums is a disgrace to a stokehold. I'm dependin' on you, Plunket,' he sez, 'and I'll ask you here and now to give me your word you'll give me a full head of steam.' 'I will, sir,' sez I, for what did I care, havin' given my word already not to do it.

"A smart feller, old McKinney. You'd think to see us sweatin' at the fires our hearts was in it to give him the steam he wanted. It's the way you trims and slices does it, for you can run the slice in without lettin' the coal down on it, keepin' it smothered in clinkers.

"Not a word says old McKinney. He just stood there lookin' at us a while, and gives a nod and turns his back, and goes up the engine-room ladders to the bridge. What he says to the captain I don't know, but what the captain sez to him I do, for the quartermaster heard him. 'They won't give me steam, won't they?' sez he. 'Then I'll give them hell.'

"It was night, you'll mind, and we was on the straight run for Cuba, with Yucatan on the starboard bow, and the old devil turns her nose at the word and runs her slap ashore. . . .

"She was insured, of course, and he is part owner of

her and his cargo is as good as ruined already, but it's
my opinion it's well we were goin' slow for all that, for
she brought up with a rip-roarin' jolt sent us flyin' all
ways, like something had sprung a steel trap under us.
What else happened down there I don't know, for I
never come up a stokehold ladder so fast in me life,
with the whole watch tryin' to climb over me at
once. . . .

"Begob, she looked a bad case on deck. Her nose
was cocked up at a big rock standin' over her port bow,
and her stern was spouting water like a tide rock, and
the passengers was burstin' out of her and fightin' their
way up the bridge ladders.

"There was a lad named Butchal was mate of mine
in the port watch, an' him an' me goes up on the
fo'castle head, where the officers and crew is, seein' what
means there is of gettin' the crowd off her. By this and
that they rigged out a spar with a tackle to it the height
of that big rock, the idea bein' to swing off on top of it
and get a hawser across. Then sez the first officer to
us all, 'I'll go first, but I'll need a couple of hands
with me to make fast the rope, so who'll volunteer?'
'We will,' sez I. 'So you should, you bastards that is
the cause of all this trouble,' sez he.

"A handy feller he was, and gives a kick off on the
end of that rope landed him on the rock. Fourteen
feet it was from the ship's side. I goes next, and begob, it was like swingin' on nothin' over a pothole in
hell with all that pother of seas below, but the First
grabs me as I come over and lands me on all fours.

Butchal followed, and they sent us over a line that got us a crowbar and a twelve-pound hammer across and we fixed the hawser fast. By that they had a flare goin' on the fo'castle head and sends the passengers over. The crew and officers come next. . . .

" 'Twas on the mainland we were, but too dark to move till dawn, and all was huddled on that rock waitin' for it. I has a look over them, and sez I to one of the crew:

" 'What's come of the firemen?' sez I.

" 'They're havin' a booze up on deck,' sez he.

" 'And us out of it,' sez I.

" 'Come back,' sez the First, 'she'll break up any minute.'

" 'She'll last a drink or two,' sez I.

" 'Come on, then,' sez he, 'I could do with one me-self.'

"A sporty feller he was. And back the three of us goes. And a night we made of it, sittin' on the fore hatch and drinkin' what we pleased. By dawn the old girl is near hogbacked in two, and the joke is we are all so boozed they has to send a relief party over to lug us out of her. . . ."

Carrol drowsed contentedly, listening to Pat's tales. An autobiographical passion was here; a frustrated literary idiom, that strung life on words with a greater gusto than by which it was lived.

Sadie twisted on her couch, cut off the while from surf and sun baking. Her eye threatened explosions, and it was better for the general ease when she went off to a privacy of hers in the scrub where there was a rock pool to sluice herself in after bathing. Like the little beach, this area was assigned to her.

Gibble spent most of the afternoon making a brush-wood seat for her at the cooking place, where the evening meal was spread on a tray of flat bark, table-clothed with leaves. His solicitude of eye for the sufferer was such that Sadie plumped into his seat-offering and disorganized it at once.

"Beastly day, hot and sticky. I'm all grass seeds, too, down my back and up my legs and in my hair and —Fish! Without salt! No, not that one, they're all bones. Do take that stick out of my back. Why don't we get schnapper here; there ought to be schnapper. I haven't the slightest appetite . . ."

She beat them with complaints; ate and rejected food, and wriggling in her seat, demanded consolation in order to denounce it.

"Ships! Don't talk of ships! Preposterous! What would ships come here for? If they knew the place existed they'd keep away from it. I won't stand it! Waiting, waiting! And nothing to wait for. I'll go mad! I'll drown myself! It's an easy death. We may never leave this place—live here for ever missing everything. We've got a new car since I've been away, a thirty-eight—ninety Vauxhall. I was dying to try it and I suppose my sister Fanny's out in it this minute, the sneak. She always got the best of everything. Why on earth didn't I go home by Suez instead of taking the American trip? Those dresses I bought in

New York! I had one lovely thing of ivory satin crêpe with gold threads and a gold satin lining. I'll never wear it now, never! It's at the bottom of the sea. I wish I was there with it . . ."

At a tragic crescendo she wept violently and got rid of her exasperation by an excess of it. When she threw herself into her crazy bed it was with an effect of collapse into instant sleep.

"She's right, of course," said Carrol, scowling at the fire. "So was Sam Johnson. 'Sir, a waste of life.' Think of never seeing *Tristan und Isolde* again! Hell!"

"Or Brown Street in the Broomilaw," said Pat with a scowl.

Sadie had left them the exploded attack of her nerves. Pat sat trickling sand through his fingers. Gibble cast a nervous glance over his shoulder at the dark sea, and returned it hastily to the fire. Carrol took out Sadie's cigarette case, in which one cigarette remained. A fear of using up one last pleasure kept it there and he thrust the case back into his pocket.

"A waste of life," he repeated. "Hell, I don't mind wasting life but this isn't even a life to waste. It's nothing; it's a vacuum; it's—For God's sake tell me one of those dam' yarns of yours, Pat."

Like a machine always wound up Pat began, "Did I ever tell you—" and stopped. "Sure I have the need on me tonight for a sup of liquor," he said mildly.

"So have I. But anyway, Pat, you don't get liquor

stoking between ports; you can do a good stretch without it."

"You've hit it there, but stokin' uses up the need for it. And then you have the grand thought behind your head you'll be in port this time so long with a pocketful of cash and the girls comin' down on the wharves to help you spend it. The worst of this place, as the girl says, is waitin' for nothin' to happen. I've been in prisons where you was better off for booze and wimmen. You doubt I'm lyin', but it's the truth I tell you. Where was it, sez you? Sure at Tampico in the Gulf of Mexico. I was four years on that coast, and that time in an old tub called the *Vittoria* out of Glasgow, chartered between Tampico, Vera Cruz and Norfolk, Virginia. A bitch she was to fire, sweatin' the life out of you to give her steam, and that was the reason we made it up between us to leave her. At Euzelia it was we give her the slip, three mile this side of Tampico, a place we discharged coke at. Me and Butchal it was that got drinkin' the stuff they calls Canya in them parts and the johndarmes run us in for a bit of a noise we made in a mud hut by this Butchal burstin' a melon on the head of a dago was interferin' with him about a wench for some unknown reason. And that's how we come by as nice a booze-up as you could wish, for we had plenty of dollars on us and a leather-faced dago with a gun to run the rabbit for us. Begob, he shoved a couple of girls in the cell for a bit over the price of them. It's good eatin' they are, them dago wenches, and this Butchal was as randy as a stopped-up billy-goat. . . .

"In the end old Captain Roberts paid our fines. A cunnin' old bastard he was, with not a fireman to be got on the beach, and me an' Butchal was the pick of the port watch. 'Come aboard now,' sez he, 'and I'll give you a bottle of whisky on top of the rubbish you are drinkin' here.' We went on board, of course, to have the laugh of him by takin' his whisky and gettin' back to the girls at Tampico: But it's him has the laugh on us, for while we are below drinkin' the officers stokes the ship up and takes her out on us. Dithered we has already by the booze we had ashore not to notice it. 'We'll be gettin' ashore now, Captain Roberts, and thanks for your whisky,' sez we when the bottle is empty. 'You'll be gettin' to the stokehold for a pair of skulkin' hodmen,' says he. 'I'll have that whisky out of your hides before we reach Norfolk, Virginia. . . .'

"Sure it's queer," said Pat irrelevantly, "me head keeps naggin' at me I must have a sup of drink this minute——"

CHAPTER SIX.

NEXT morning Pat led Carrol off along the
beach with an air of purpose, and there, by
the aid of a stick, gave a very exact performance of how a gun should be shouldered, ported,
stood at ease, and brought to the salute.

He then did the bayonet exercise with great vigour. . . .

These demonstrations of a disciplined earth seemed to have a reviving effect on him.   He was very jaunty after them, squaring his shoulders and stepping up briskly to lend a hand where required.   For the afternoon, he had Carrol off in quest of fruit.   They came back late to the camp with an armful of plantains, which revived optimism all round.   Roasted on stones, they added another cooked dish to the island menu.

With that Pat appeared to have used up the resources of a life too idle.   On the reef next morning he took sudden offence over a theory of tying on hooks, and lost two to prove himself in the wrong about it. And as rejecting further opinion on the matter he threw the line after them and stamped off the reef to vanish in the scrub.

"He's got nerves, the old blighter," said Carrol.

"He's got no patience," said Gibble.   "We can't afford to lose hooks like that.   And he talks too much —scares the fish away. . . ."

Pat came out of the scrub at midday with a smouldering eye, which rejected inquiry into its motives for rejecting inquiry.   He sat down at the cooking place and at once found food a cause for offence.

"To hell with eatin'," he said, taking a bite at a plantain and throwing it away.

"Have a drink, then," said Carrol, handing a coconut.

"Put it down or I'll knock the head off you with it," roared Pat, leaping up.

All stared at a palpable lunatic. Pat glared back at them as at a congress gathered to hear of wrongs.

"Am I not out of my mind with drinkin' the juice of them things?" he shouted. "A man has his needs and to hell with the lie in it. Is it reason would have him goin' round with a head on him like a pig's bladder stuffed with wind and a cravin' in his guts for a sup of liquor to make him see the fun of goin' on livin' at all? The horrors is sense to a place like this. I'd call it luck to be in old Mother Cregan's boardin' house in Brown Street off the Broomilaw with nothin' on me but an old quilt, near dead with the drink, and the old woman and her daughter Minnie fryin' eggs for me in the pan, never thinkin' with the shakes and trembles on me I'd be cursin' the time I stand here this minute with the drouth on me of bein' sober."

He raised a fist and shook it in anathema at the cloudless sky, his voice pitched to the chant of a despairing litany.

"May the almighty curse of God rest on old Joe Plunket and Mary Gavan for puttin' me in this hole of a world to end livin' in it out of sight or sense of good liquor that is the only thing worth livin' in it for."

It seemed to Carrol that these ravings should be put in order. Therefore, he stood up with an air that assumed them disposed of and said: "Sit down, Pat. Be a sensible fool and eat your tucker."

Pat waved an arm at the earth which rejected it for

ever. He then shut his eyes, screwed up his face and gritted his teeth. If these were exercises to control despair, they failed to control it. On opening his eyes he straightway gave Carrol a punch in the ribs that put him out of action with fearful effect.

"Will you talk to me that cannot bear the breath of reason on me?" he shouted.

Carrol sat down and took gaping mouthfuls of air. It was a full minute before the powers of articulation were restored to him in a burst of fury.

"You infernal old hound!" he yelled.

"Am I not in grief this minute?" roared Pat.

"I wish you were in the lagoon, you bloody old maniac."

"You ought to be thoroughly ashamed of yourself," said Sadie indignantly.

"You ought, you really ought to control yourself," said Gibble.

Pat made a distracted gesture.

"Not one of you has a heart of feelin' in you," he shouted, and stamped off across the beach to vanish, with a final anathema at sea and sky, 'round the headland.

He left a highly outraged convention behind him, and a topic exhilarated by indignant repetition.

"He must be made to understand that he *must* control himself," insisted Gibble.

"He needs putting in his place," said Sadie.

"He needs stunning with a lump of rock," said Carrol.

He felt his ribs gingerly, to be quite sure that one or two were not broken.

"I doubt physical violence would be effective," said Gibble. "We should apply moral suasion."

"I prefer a policy of direct action. If he comes that caper again I intend to have a lump of rock handy."

Theories of preserving decorum were not pressed into service because Pat remained out of sight, and Carrol and Gibbie became quite friendly that afternoon. They took fishing lines and went down to the flat rocks below the headland that separated the two beaches. Sadie was again free of the water and returned to it gladly. Her beach was hidden from the flat rocks, but when she swam out to the reef, Carrol turned to watch the warm tint of her body in the surf, which Gibble carefully refrained from seeing. He was still busy over Pat's outbreak, which had seriously disturbed him.

"The point is, don't you think you encourage him too much listening to those stories of his?" he said.

"Lord, no, I find them most amusing."

"Amusing?"

"Yes. It's always been a puzzle to me where the illiterate get their trick of telling a yarn constructively. Pat doesn't know what an anticlimax is, but he uses it perfectly. Educate Pat and he wouldn't be able to tell a yarn or use a single sentence that wasn't a commonplace. There's no doubt that education destroys whatever intelligence the people have——"

"No, no; what I meant was, encouraging him by not

trying to correct him for a loose moral outlook; he appears to have done the most brutal things . . ."

"Correct him? What do you take me for, Gibby? I don't care a tinker's curse what the old blighter's done."

"You don't?"

"Of course, I don't. Nor do you, or anyone else. People who raise objections to the acts of others are only confessing a fear of doing the same things themselves."

"You don't object to getting a violent blow from that—that—that Irishman?"

"By thunder, I do. But don't think you've got me there because you haven't. It's a crude fact that life as a personal experience can be dull, ugly, brutal, painful, silly, and all the rest of it, but all these things become fascinating as a tale told about somebody else. Of course, I object to getting a punch in the ribs from Pat, but I don't object to hearing him tell about punching other people's ribs. In fact, I enjoy it."

"You do?"

"I do. And so do you."

"I do not."

"If I had any daily paper here I'd soon settle that. You'd do what everybody else does, turn to the last horrible murder and read every detail of it. Didn't you know it was one of the standing jokes of journalism to say that the people of Sydney were horrified at the ghastly crime when we know that the whole mob are gloating over it?"

"I won't accept such a word. It's not so. I'm convinced that I, and all decent people, read of such things with horror."

"That's only a blind for fascination. If they really horrified you, you couldn't bear to read them. I'm not saying it's wrong to be fascinated by brutal deeds; I only say that they fascinate. Nice kind deeds don't fascinate. Do you think we'd dare headline a pretty love affair with the same attention to details that we give a murder? If we did, we'd have every wowser in the country howling at us. But give them two columns of murdered corpse and they fairly lap up the blood."

Gibble suffered a contraction of the stomach which caused him to shudder.

"You say horrible things," he protested.

"Lord, Gibby, you join the staff of a paper and you won't say there's anything horrible about murder; it's a most meritorious act, beloved by the people. The only horrible, vile, indecent, disgusting act is the act of love; we're never allowed to mention it. . . ."

A nice embarrassment in popular morality was scattered there by Carrol exclaiming, "Hello, I've got a bite," and he became intent on the art of fisherman. Gibble went further along the reef to try a cast; this talking disturbed the fish. . . .

From there he could see Sadie's head as she swam into the surf that creamed over the reef. Once she drew herself up on a rock to turn over backwards with a golden flash of legs and arms. In a hurry Gibble turned attention back to his line.

The afternoon shadows stippled the beaches and with the sun in her eyes it was some time before Sadie discovered that Pat had come out on her beach and was studying her antics in the water with a connoisseur's detachment. She waved him off at once. With a friendly wave that disposed of concern on his account, Pat walked at leisure to where her clothes lay and sat down by them.

Sadie was instantly in a temper. Caprice in being approached renounced approach that blackmailed her nudity in those terms. She swam straight to where the beach allowed her to stand neck deep in the water and nodded Pat an imperious dismissal from the beach.

"You get away from there; I'm coming out," she called.

"Isn't that what I'm waitin' for?" said Pat.

"Damned cheek; do you think I'm coming out with you grinning there?"

"Why shouldn't you, with a figure on you any girl would be proud to be seen in?"

"Do as you're told at once."

"I'll feed out of your hand for the askin'," said Pat, making no attempt to go.

Their voices had reached the flat rocks and Carrol and Gibble appeared round the headland, staring.

"Will you clear out?" they heard Sadie demand fiercely.

Pat grinned at her. In a rage, she dived, swam out in a circle and back again. The exercise exhilarated her temper; with slapping knees she strode out of the

water to where her clothes lay and snatched them up. Pat reached out an easy movement that caught a polished leg and pulled her over on top of him.

"Give me a kiss and it's all I'll ask," said he.

The kiss he took, and got with it a slap that would have stunned a lesser man. Sadie wrenched herself free and whipped on her petticoat and chemise.

"Idiot!" she said, and walked off austerely.

"You're as bad as them others for havin' no joy in you at all," called Pat after her, with pardonable annoyance.

Sadie passed Carrol and Gibble with a pair of magnificent breasts that threatened to explode her chemise.

"Impertinent old fool," was her comment to their stare of inquiry into opinion on this event. . . .

She left on the air a sweet aroma from her sea and sun scented body, and Carrol gazed after her, admiring the imperious sway of her thighs modelled in a damp petticoat. Impossible not to endorse Pat's tribute to these graces. Gibble was quite confounded by an act of irreverence for them as he stared from Sadie back to Pat, who now sat moodily on the beach, trickling sand through his fingers.

"Tut tut tut! this won't do at all.   This is—this is—really, this is too much," he said.

"Well, I think Sadie had the best of that round.   At the same time Pat is a bit of a problem."

"He's thoroughly irresponsible. We must take measures to see that this sort of thing doesn't occur again."

"Well, what measures . . ."

But Sadie was very contemptuous of opinion on that score. She came out of her scrub privacy that evening with her hair combed and plaited and decorated with hibiscus blossoms and about her the refreshing effect of a careful toilet.

"I know how to keep *that* fool in his place," she said.

"I believe it," said Carrol, admiring the limpid strength of her bare arms.

Pat was still absent when they cooked the evening meal. Gibble cleaned the fish which Sadie and Carrol grilled on stones before the fire. Plantains were roasted too, and a gracious odour went forth on the calm air. Perhaps it induced Pat to reflect on the mistake of imposing octracism on himself, for he now approached the camp gravely, inviting attention to the expression of one aware of spiritual amendments.

"Miss Sadie, will you look me in the eye a minute?" he said.

"Pooh!" said Sadie, and added to Carrol, "Pass the fish."

"Miss Sadie," went on the pacifist solemnly, "the words I have to say to you is these. For intrusion when at your bath I ask your pardon."

"So you should," said Sadie briefly.

The envoy of contrition then turned to Carrol.

"Jimmy lad, the words I have to say to you is these. For the thump I give you in passin' this mornin' I ask your pardon."

"I give it conditionally; don't do it again," said Carrol.

"On the word of honour of a man that never broke his word to friend or foe, the words I have to say this minute are, 'Never will I do it again.'" He then added, "Gibby, lad, your hand," and shook Gibble's limp paw in the heartiest manner.

"And now, you fulsome old hound, sit down and eat the food you came for," said Carrol.

"Never think it of me," said Pat, taking a generous allowance of fish. "Not food, but friendliness has brought me here. I am a man could never bear the hankerin' after ill feelin's once blows is done with. Let what is past be bygones and forgotten."

"No, but I mean it. Next time you lose your temper, go and punch a palm tree."

"I will, I will, never be unaisy in your mind about it. 'Twas no more than the pop of a cork on a hot day."

"Kick of a horse, you mean."

"For an unforgivin' nature you mind me of a Glebe Island butcher I lodged with in Sydney be the name of Peter Coolan. A suspicious, treacherous feller he was, for a man married to as fine a girl you'd wish to get your arm round. 'Twas not in harm but nature that her and me would be friendly in the house with Peter away all day workin' at the Island, but whether or not it was the neighbours talkin', or the man's natural unforgivin' nature, or him comin' in one evenin' I am givin' her a bit of a hug in the wash-house, but he ups with a pick handle and gives me a clout on the skull with it. He has himself to blame for the latherin' I give him for that, but there was no ill feelin' in it, and all shakes hands after as nice as you could wish. Will you believe me when I tell you that same man has me laid for next night by three Glebe Island butchers not includin' him-

self and well-nigh kicks the stuffin' out of me for good. Is that an unforgivin' nature or is it not?"

"I should call it the reasoned policy of a husband who has a boarder like you in the house. The only mistake about it was bringing three butchers. He ought to have brought ten, and a shotgun."

"It's not what you think or you'd never have the heart to say it," said Pat, satisfied at having presented himself as a harmless fellow depreciated by hard-hearted butchers.

Again, the graces of a social gathering. Pat reclined at ease, exuding a generous warmth to all. Gibble fussed about Sadie's seat putting it in order for her. Carrol went through his usual performance of taking out his cigarette, looking at it, and putting it away again.

"I like to think it's there," he said. "I can have a smoke if I want to. But the queer thing is I'm beginning not to want to. I don't believe I've thought of a smoke all day."

"The same with me, though I never thought of it till this minute," said Pat surprised.

"For deprivations we no longer feel deprived of let us be thankful. . . ."

Carrol stretched himself on his back at Sadie's feet and gazed contentedly up at the stars. A phrase of music floated across his mind and he hummed it aloud.

"Hallo! That's the horn theme from the second act of *Tristan und Isolde*. What put that into my mind, I wonder? The blue depth of night, per-haps——"

But his eye left the blue depth of night to travel up Sadie's figure; over the plumped bare knees, the resolute breasts thrusting two bronze plaits to left and right, up the column of her throat, squared at either angle of the jaw, to rest on the broad pattern of lips, and the reposeful heavy eyelids.

"There's something Wagnerian about you, Sadie," he said.

"Of course, I was *taught* singing," admitted Sadie.

"I should like to hear you sing Brunnhilde's song of greeting to the dawn."

"I used to sing a good deal of *Madame Butterfly*. And *La Bohême*, of course."

"Of course."

"I wish you'd sing something now," urged Gibble.

"I couldn't, without music."

"Do, Sadie," said Carrol.

"Do, I beg," said Gibble.

"Do, an' please the lot of us," said Pat.

Sadie hummed a bar or two. "I forget the words; I never could remember the words of grand opera——" She hummed other matters, with a sentimental eye on vacancy, adding, "Perhaps I could remember the 'Indian Lullaby.'"

All reclined expectantly; Sadie preened her fine figure, sweeping detachment down at a vast audience; the song was sung.

Carrol watched a singing throat, soothed by facile

fooleries issuing from it.   Gibble listened with the transferred vision of a patient under hypnosis.   Pat lolled, with a maudlin eye on the stars.

"Lovely!—lovely!" breathed Gibble, as the song ended.

"You make me think I'm in Naples harbour with the stars shinin' and the street singers comin' down on the wharves an' all," said Pat sentimentally.

Sadie swept a downward glance at Carrol, who was ready with his tribute too.

"You undoubtedly have a grand opera contralto, Sadie," he said firmly.

In short, it was a most successful evening, though nobody knew exactly why.

CHAPTER SEVEN

F OR all your talk, you'll admit there's aggravation havin' a wench about your eye all day and
no proper use made of her," said Pat.

"Well, yes," admitted Carrol. "All the same, it
hasn't bothered me much on this island."

"You're either lyin', or you haven't got it to bother
you."

"Of course, I have. I'm never without the thought
of a woman somewhere at the back of my mind. But
it won't work here, Pat. I've thought it out, and I'm
determined to look at the situation with a cold eye.
On every count, there'd be hell to pay. For a start,
the three of us would be as mad as snakes with each
other in no time."

"There's where your suspicious nature comes in; for
why should not the lot of us agree in friendliness and
reason?"

"There's no such thing as reason in any affair where

a woman is involved and as for friendliness—No, I wouldn't trust you, you old blighter; you do your block in too easily."

"I give you the lie; a kinder man never breathed."

"All right, you're a noble-hearted fellow. But what we would do in such a situation is a side issue. Think of the other consequences. . . . No, in plain flat terms it *won't do*, Pat, so shut up about it."

He got up from sun-baking and stretched himself, gazing with some complacence over his tanned body.

"I'm putting on weight and getting some decent form into my muscles," he said. "Blast these whiskers; I wish we had a razor."

"I'll say they give you a bit of a look of a dago," said Pat impartially.

"You look like a damned old pirate yourself."

"Come and spar with me a bit; it's exercise we both need."

Sadie came round the headland from her beach, passing the two naked boxers at the water's edge. Gibble was staggering up to the camp with a load of firewood, and frowned at a general disregard for the proprieties. It was very annoying that he could not get the others to regulate their bathing hours, and they were daily getting slacker of reservations when Sadie was about. The worst of it was that Sadie never seemed to be aware that an awful deference should be made to her eyesight. At a hint from her, Gibble would have made a path to her beach through the scrub, but he never got the hint. . . .

It was a relief now when she disappeared into her scrub privacy, with that Irishman turkey-cocking about the beach with an inflated chest and a military jauntiness of bearing.

"There's Lady Sadie gone to take a peep at us from the bushes," he said to Carrol with satisfaction.

"You are an idealist and an exhibitionist," said Carrol.

"I am a grand figure of a man," said Pat.

"Then come and give Gibby a hand with the firewood. He has his eye on you for a low fellow with no proper respect for ladies."

"He has what all them parsons has, and that's a dread in his eye for what decent people calls fun. But sure, there never was a man yet would be a creepin' Jasus in a black coat."

He was, therefore, especially hearty with his "Gibby lads" when they pulled on a pair of pants each and went to assist with the firewood.

There was always something to do in the mornings, but their afternoons moved to an idle beat. With the midday meal over an effect of drivelling beset their minds, not unpleasant, but not a distinctive state of being.

In that state they now sat about the camp, and no one bothered to talk. An unconscious social economy was practised there, for if they used up too much talk during the day there was a lack of it in the evening. An existence incessantly threatened by boredom must learn not to squander its few resources. . . .

Gibble got up first, by the inveterate attraction of pottering. He had some fibres soaking in a coconut shell of water and he went off to tie them between prongs of wood, so that they would stretch in drying. Pat rose to yawn and scratch and expand his chest as he moved off down the beach to the deep shade of a banyan, where he stretched out and went to sleep. He had acquired the habit of the siesta.

Carrol and Sadie sat on at the camp, though neither was aware of an obligation to entertain each other, which is one way of confessing intimacy. Sadie squatted on the sand with her elbows on her knees and her head laid sideways on one arm and her eyes magnetized drowsily on the line of foam at the reef. That was always an attraction to the eyes and Carrol watched it too. He was seated above her on one of their crude seats and his knee touched the rich curve of her back. Perhaps her back touched his knee. At any rate, he became abruptly conscious of her upturned cheek and the coral tint of her ear, and bent down to kiss it.

Nothing in that, of course, and Sadie made nothing of it. She did not even move her head, so Carrol had to slip a hand under her chin to tilt it and kiss her lips upside down. She let him have them without consent or protest, though his beard tickled her nose, which made a novel caress of it, as she had never been kissed by a beard before. Carrol said, "Damn these whiskers," and sat up in a hurry, because Gibble was coming back from the scrub, though Sadie made nothing of that either. It was Carrol who moved swiftly apart from her, while she only returned her languid gaze to the surf. "I find that coconut palm fibres strip best," said Gibble brightly, and showed a specimen to Carrol, who expressed a lively interest in it. He joined Gibble at once in lengthening their fishing lines. Sadie discovered that her hair was sticky from too much salt water, and loitered off to wash it in her rock pool. . . .

Carrol was an honest fellow; he had to be, under the circumstances. When he told Pat that competition for the possession of Sadie would not do, he meant it. That is perhaps one of the best ways of hiding ill-advised proposals from oneself. He was also a wise fellow, and perceived that what stability their life possessed rested on him. Pat and Gibble could communicate through him but not to each other, while he had an idiom for both of them and Sadie too. All social disruption begins by the gracious practise of love, and there would be uproars at once if he put in a superior claim to its rewards on that infernal island, where each was exposed to a microscopic inspection by the others. And if he started fooling with Sadie he would not be able to stop. But he had started fooling with her.— Dilemma! . . .

He went off fishing with Gibble in a very disturbed state of mind, because to the wise precautions of analysis he was constantly thinking of the sweet taste of Sadie's lips, and threw in his line without baiting it. Apprised of this oversight after a fruitless interval, he baited and cast again, and at the first nibble gave a violent tug that lost both hook and fish. Clearly he was not in trim for fishing. . . .

"These hooks are no good except for small fish," he said, vacillating over tying on a new one. "I wonder how the links of that fan chain of Sadie's would work?"

"Good idea; I never thought of it," said Gibble.

"I'll go and try it, anyway."

He walked slowly back to the camp, meditating between footsteps. The exercise he made there of combing his hair with his fingers was mere aberration, since it was very long, and for appearance otherwise, he wore nothing but a pair of disreputable linen trousers.

Two paths were already worn from the camp into the scrub, one to their water supply and the other to Sadie's rock pool. It was really a privacy, banked in by massed foliage and draped in creepers, and Carrol stopped in the scrub to call, "Are you in there, Sadie?"

"Yes."

"Can I come into your house?"

"Wait half a minute."

When Carrol emerged she had pulled on her petticoat and chemise and was seated with her hair fluffed out in the sunlight, drying it.

"I'm after that fan chain of yours to try it for fish-hooks," explained Carrol.

"Take it, of course."

The chain lay on a sheet of bark with her fan and rings and bracelets and her wristlet watch, which she had given up winding; the system for which it ticked off a routine had vanished over the sea rim.

Carrol took the chain and sat down beside Sadie and began to detach a link. It excused the slight ill-ease that premeditation bestows on these affairs. Sadie went on combing her hair, which picked up lambent ripples from sun splashes through the creepers above. This occupation soothed her discontented eyelids as stroking a cat's fur sends it to sleep. Carrol gave up fiddling with the chain to watch her, finding her a charming spectacle.

"You have lovely hair, Sadie."

"Salt water doesn't improve it."

"Incredible, the way modern women have sacrificed their hair. It's a species of funk, or a concession to homosexuality."

He took a handful of this inspiring hair to arrange it over her forehead and admire the effect.

"I have worn it done up, for fancy dress," said Sadie.

"Suits you, any way you do it. I like it down best."

He drew the bronzed mass smoothly round her cheeks and in that setting the compactly built face with tinted eyelids, wide nostrils and embossed scarlet lips was very attractive and he kissed the lips.

"At last year's Artists' Ball in Sydney I went as a woman of the eighties," said Sadie. "You know, tight stays, a bustle and a long-trained skirt, and my hair done up on top, with curls down the back. Everyone said it suited me."

"It would," said Carrol, kissing her again.

"Rotten for dancing in, though, those long skirts," said Sadie, talking through his kiss.

Her lips, so boldly modelled that they looked hard, were delightfully soft to kiss. Carrol took possession of them till with a sudden stiffening of their tissues she withdrew them.

"A nuisance, all the same, not having a water-proof cap for surfing," she remarked, going on with her hair.

"Hang it, Sadie, let your hair alone; I want to kiss you," complained Carrol.

Sadie went on doing her hair. Her disconcerting content was expressed by a self-contained attention to her own actions and a disregard for Carrol's. She did not mind him kissing her but she did not stop doing her hair, so he was forced to endure the toilet interval by kissing her shoulders and the back of her neck. Even when the hair was neatly plaited and disposed of he was not much better off because Sadie at once returned his hand to him and rolled him over on his back and tickled his ribs, which Carrol could not bear, and was forced to gasp frantic protests for fear of alarming the beach by yells for mercy.

Still, it was good, if disturbing fun, and they still sprawled and chatted and sometimes wrestled an hour later, and Carrol got quite a shock to hear Gibble's voice calling from the beach.

He snatched a farewell from Sadie's lips, commanding caution with a gesture as he slid off into the bush, to reappear well down the beach, and from there approach the camp.

"How did it go?" asked Gibble with interest.

"Eh?" said Carrol, alarmed.

"The chain, for hooks."

"Oh, that.   I couldn't find Sadie."

"Why, I can hear her in there."

Sadie, in fact, was humming a contralto passage in the scrub.

"She must have got back; I'll ask her now."

He strolled off, and Gibble heard him ask Sadie for the chain.   What he did not hear was the kiss that acknowledged Carrol's wink in exchange for it.   Humming, Carrol returned working at a link with the nail file.

There was a certain smugness about Carrol and Sadie that night round the fire, well disguised by Carrol's frank interest in conversation with Pat and Gibble, who undoubtedly participated in currents of self-esteem going round the circle, for they found Sadie a very rare spectacle, perched up on her brushwood throne with her prima donna's chest and her contralto voice.

She sang, by fervent request, and Carrol relaxed as sentimentally as the others over music for the drawing-room. . . .

But he rationalized the event to himself when all had retired to their lairs.   A trifle, after all.   Sadie clearly regarded it as a trifle, too, which was a relief.   Also an aggravation.   He kept craning his ear across the dim space of sand in starlight to listen for signals of her presence, but heard none. She had magnificent powers of sleep. The others slept too. Carrol only remained awake, such is the annoyance of lyricism in the blood.

"Damn this," he said at last. "It won't do, submitting to emotional thrills. It won't do. . . ."

CHAPTER EIGHT

IS IT fruitin' you are goin' this mornin' or is it that
you are not goin' fruitin'?" asked Pat, in terms of
forensic nicety.

Carrol sat up where he sprawled in the sand and
appeared to reflect over a choice of alternatives.

100

"How are we off for lines?" he asked Gibble.

"We have enough to go on with."

"All right, I'll get guavas and Pat can get plantains; it's too long to go both ways in one journey."

"But there are guavas close here, over by that bent palm," said Gibble.

"Not ripe. No more jokes with unripe guavas for me. The ripe ones are in that gully half a mile from here."

"You know best," said Gibble.

The fruit gatherers went their ways and Gibble returned to his morning job of laying the fire and collecting wood. They had rolled a fallen tree to the cooking place, and this required adjusting as it slowly burned away. Gibble was now expert in calculating the burning capacity of woods, but he disliked going too far from the fire, which the others left entirely to him, by his express request. He distrusted their probity for a responsibility of that sort. The stability of their existence rested on him, he was well aware. His was the wisdom to forecast, the industry to pursue. Incessant pottering matured a great consciousness of worth in him. He did not sun-bake and squander hours in the water like the others. A morning swim, and the day's work was before him. Besides, he exercised a moral restraint. Not perhaps so actively as he could have wished, but at least by a tacit rejection of loose conduct. If he did not protest at laxities of talk between Carrol and that Irishman, he refused to endorse them. It was sufficient.

Now, doing his best to break up wood into sizable lengths, he suffered conscience pangs over those two axes that had gone down in the boat. A criminal oversight not to have grabbed up one at the last moment. The services of that kind God were clearly indicated here in the character of a providential ironmonger.

Sadie appeared from her bush alcove, loitering through the sun-splashed shadows. Like the others she had permanently discarded shoes, and her strong shapely legs were bare under her kilt of a petticoat. With a chemise, it was all she ever wore. Her dress, stockings and pants were folded between two pieces of bark and placed carefully away in a hollow log. Potency had been deleted from a frustrated symbol for drapers' shops by a freed body which wished to discard clothes altogether. Even Gibble, who was never seen outside his trousers, was no longer embarrassed to be seen only in his trousers.

"Swimming?" he inquired brightly.

"Of course."

"Lovely morning for a swim."

It depressed Gibble that he always fell into banalities of that sort when alone with Sadie. When by himself he was able to express himself as a very entertaining fellow, full of diverting topics. He dredged for one now.

"I've been thinking; the natives of these islands make a sort of cloth out of bark. We might experiment with it."

"Bark! It sounds horrible."

"I believe it can be softened and made quite pliable. I've read of it, but can't recall how it's done."

"Oh, we'll all be dressed in a fig leaf before long." She moved off to her beach, leaving Gibble again depressed over his inability to interest her. He began to hurry on with his jobs so that he would be free to go fishing on the reef.

Carrol had stated that the guavas near the camp were unripe, but that was not true. He went straight to them and gathered a quantity in his coat, which he carried through the bush to Sadie's beach. Sadie had just arrived there. She was standing at the water's edge, stripped, with her face turned to the scrub, watching it. At Carrol's appearance she waved briefly and waded in to swim strongly out to the reef. From there she could be seen from the other beach and command privacy for her bathing interval. Now she swam straight back and emerged to slap the water from her body with a freedom that charmed Carrol, though she qualified it a little by slipping on her petticoat before crossing the beach to Carrol.

"Why do you bother to put that rag on, Sadie?"

"You wear trousers."

"But shame is man's disgrace; women don't know it exists."

He pulled her into his arms and began to kiss her with inspired ardour. It was the simmering factor of his being those days, and Sadie encouraged it and defeated it on a nicely balanced system of frustration. She must have come straight from Olympus to practise such a wretched trick. That notable capacity for concentrating attention on her own affairs made nothing of Carrol's proposal to share them too. . . .

"But, Sadie, adorable girl, nice girl, kind girl, listen a moment and stop exerting that brute strength of yours. I've got something important to say to you.—Trust me."

"Trust you for what?"

"To be careful."

"Oh, of course, careful."

"I swear I will be. Hang it, Sadie, I wouldn't take a risk in this place for any consideration. That's obvious; we mustn't take risks. Consequently, we're safe. You simply can't go wrong by trusting me."

"Well, I won't."

She gave him an open-mouthed kiss which shot them both with electric aggressions. Great fun, these wrestling matches, and the most exasperating things on earth. And Sadie was mean enough to resort to tickling at a crisis, which caused Carrol to collapse on the spot, gasping frenzied protests.

"Bitch—torturess—I hate you. You've got a base mind. What's worse, you're as strong as a horse. I always hated strong girls; they degrade the whole theory of male dominance. Why can't you be a modest girl; a nice tender trusting girl . . . ?"

"Thanks, I'm not one of those idiots."

"You are an idiot; you don't know the first principle of feminine ruthlessness. The secret of subjecting the male is a pose of meek submission. It was practised by our grandmothers and look at the awful things they did to our grandfathers.   But honestly, Sadie, enough of this crude horse-play; it never gives me a chance to tell you how deeply, passionately, devotedly I love you."

He ranged up beside her and smoothed her cheek, and placed a tender respectful kiss on her brow.

"Trust me, beloved," he said.

Sadie relieved herself of him to flick her damp hair about and dry it.   She liked its soft caress against her bare back.

"A nice idiot I'd be, getting into a mess in a place like this.   Careful!   Oh, yes, careful.   My sister Fanny got nicely tripped up that way last year, though she and her boy were frightfully careful.   She swore he was and so did he but how *can* you tell—It wasn't so much getting her fixed up; her boy arranged that; it was the awful trouble of getting away from home for a fortnight.   We had to arrange a trip to Melbourne in our car.   She didn't go, of course, but I went with a friend, so that I could post letters home which she wrote beforehand to prove she was there.   It turned out all right and nobody found out about it, but it was a frightful nuisance all the same."

"To get at the truth of this, I bet it was you who got caught and sister Fanny who went off to post the letters."

"Pooh!   Fanny always was a fool with boys.   Sentimental!   You ought to see the things she writes about them in her diary.   Drivel about devoted swooning

passion and mad ravings about their eyes and arms and the way they do their hair. You'd think they were gods or movie actors."

"All I can say is that I wish your sister Fanny had been wrecked on this island instead of you."

He lay over on his back with an elaborate pretence of having had enough of her. She was an automatic rejecter, one of those infernal girls who are able to click off an emotional disturbance at will on some system that the male mind has never been able to fathom. Moreover, she refused to pay back in kind impassioned imageries of her own desirability because she accepted them as understood.   Carrol accepted them as understood too, glancing up at her Amazon's arm, raised to toss back her hair, with its splendid deltoid flexed above a patch of gold in the armpit.   On her broad smooth shoulders there was room for a battalion of kisses.   Her breasts were always cool, and that was a male mystery.

As usual, his inspection of these magics worked their own infatuation on him and he reached over to begin a march of kisses up her back.   When he had arrived at her neck she said calmly:

"Mind, there's Gibby."

Carrol shot back like a crayfish and lay flat.   Gibble had come round the headland, ostentatiously casting a line.   The line cast, he furtively inspected the beach till his eye sought out Sadie's figure in the shade.   At once he looked away and went on with his fishing.

"Has he gone?" whispered Carrol.

"No."

"Curse him!"

"You'd better go."

"This beach is to dam' crowded.   Lean back till I kiss you."

In malice over Gibble's crouching figure down there by the rocks, she pulled Carrol over on his back, biting and tickling him and bestowing death by frenzy on him.

"Don't—for God's sake!—Hell!—I'll kill you," he hissed, fighting out of her clutches on his back and wriggling into the scrub.

"Abominable girl! Betrayer of helpless manhood—I hate you," he whispered ferociously back at her.

She only went on with that infernal hair of hers, as cool as an Undine.

Carrol gathered up his fruit and went off with it, muttering expletives at the undergrowth. As a lyrist, he required to arrive at realism in love to delete him of lyricism. He had endured a week of this sort of thing, too. . . .

The undergrowth here already showed signs of passage through it. They had learned its ways. In a glade behind the camp he came on Pat, with a bunch of plantains over his shoulder.

"Never say you've done your fruitin' so soon," said Pat.

"Eh?"

"I'm sayin' you are not so long about it as usual."

"What d'you mean? Damn it, you can't always come at ripe fruit. I happened to find these by chance."

"Of course, you did. I'm remarkin' on your doin' the job so quick."

Carrol shut up; he did not desire to discuss insinuations on that topic. Pat whistled with an elaborate parade of innocence. . . .

Sadie had returned to the water. Gibble crouched on

the flat rocks, too intently fishing. He kept his back
rigidly towards Sadie's beach so that she would be quite
sure he did not wish to glimpse her nudity. By moving
up the rocks he would not be able to do so, but an

invincible pull kept him anchored where he was, though
he contrived to evade its motive by wishing she would
not bathe naked at all. It was a dangerous incentive
to lawless proposals from that Irishman. For all one
knew the wretch was hiding in the scrub now, waiting
to see her tall golden figure emerge from the water.

Gibble had seen him the other night at the camp fire deliberately look up her skimpy petticoat. Doubtless her innocence had overlooked the elevation of her knees, but the pose must have left a most undesirable impression on that Irishman. Undesirable as a spectacle presented to that Irishman, but not as a thing in itself. Even Gibble's trick of reversing alarms in the conscious could not bring itself to admit that. In fact, he could not get that vision of plump pink limbs out of his mind, but he countered disturbing emotions on that score by the understanding that while such revelations were safe in his keeping, they were not be to trusted to that Irishman. They must demoralize that Irishman. Her innocence must be protected from that Irishman.

Carrol did not intrude at all on Gibble's proposals to exclude Sadie from dangerous possessions. Gibble now knew Carrol; a loose talker, but harmless. . . .

He gathered his catch together and stood up, with an excuse for looking across at Sadie.

"Lunch?" he called.

"No hurry," called Sadie, loafing on her back in the water.

Bearing his fish, and a vision of half-submerged girl, Gibble returned to the camp, where Carrol and Pat reclined at some distance from each other, putting in time while waiting for food. Encouraged by a slight effect of detachment between those two, Gibble lowered his voice to Carrol.

"I've been thinking: I don't quite like the idea of

Sadie bathing over there by herself, unless one of us is about to watch over her.   I mean, after that conduct of Pat's last week."

To his surprise Carrol met him there in the best spirit of Wesleyanism.

"You're quite right, the old devil's not to be trusted at all.   We'll have a talk about it later."

"Good," said Gibble heartily.

His opinion of Carrol went up immensely.

CHAPTER NINE

CARROL and Gibble had their talk together when Pat had gone off for his siesta and Sadie to her bush alcove.

Said Carrol: "Our present slipshod system leaves Pat too many loose ends. The best thing we can do is to divide the day into two watches. Sadie swims most of the morning, so if you do your fishing about the same time you can keep an eye on her from the rocks there."

"I take you—quite so."

"That will leave Pat to me for the morning, and there won't be any difficulty keeping tag on him. We'll leave wood gathering for the afternoon, which will be a good excuse for you to keep an eye on Pat. And we ought to get some constructive job going; a hut, for example."

"Certainly, that must be done."

"We'll need Pat there to pull down branches. He likes showing off his strength. Give the old devil a bit of judicious flattery . . ."

"I will; count on me for that."

"The main point about the business is that it doesn't much matter where Sadie is as long as one of us has an eye on Pat."

"Exactly."

"And if Pat isn't about, then one of us will need to keep an eye on Sadie."

"Exactly."

"At the same time Pat's a cunning old devil and it won't do to let him spot our game."

"We must be diplomatic . . ."

Gibble felt a warm regard for Carrol; he had strangely misjudged the integrity of his character.

Diplomacy, under cover of hut building, was introduced that evening round the camp fire.

"We can't expect this perfect weather to last for ever," said Gibble, "and you know that when it does rain in the tropics it's no joke. We *must* have a substantial hut. The trouble is to get enough straight timber for rafters and cross pieces. If we only had one of those axes . . ."

"We'll have to put the strong man on the job," said Carrol.

"I've done weight liftin' in me time, never a lie in it," said Pat, expanding at once. "A horse and cab, no less, for it run over me. Have I the mark of it, or have I not? This bit of a scrape on the ribs is it, I think. The horse trod on me and the cab run over me. You think I was drunk, but I was not. The cause of it was that very same beatin' I got from Peter Coolan and his mates, and comin' into George Street a bit dithered by it, this cab come to run over me. They took me to the hospital, but the joke is the feller was in the cab thinks the crack I have in the skull was come by the cab and not by Peter and his mates, and shoves a fiver in me hand, thinkin' maybe I'd be after him for damages. As good a bit of luck as ever I come by givin' that cab a lift across me chest."

"I've discovered that Pat is your perfect example of that theory of benevolence, Gibby. Anything that half kills him is a great bit of luck for not killing him."

"Of course, it is," said Pat. "That cab might have been a motor car. And I am five quid to the good for a booze-up when the doctor is done stitchin' me."

"Well, we're out of accidents here, unless you have the luck to pull a tree over on top of yourself. I'll sling you a fiver if you do, to keep the benevolent theory going."

"It's not the fiver but the pub to spend it in we need here."

"True. All the same, there's one real pull about this place; we don't have to make money here."

At that thought he took from his hip pocket the leather case that held his passport and a roll of notes. He had always carried it on shipboard for security, and had thus brought to the island a thing of least value there.

"Two-fifty," he said, glancing at the wad of notes. "Silly dam' things. I'll get even with the curse of a universal poverty complex for once, anyhow," and threw the case into the fire. Gibble instantly snatched it out again.

"Don't do that," he said, shocked.

"I never see the beat of that for foolishness," said Pat.

"Idiot," said Sadie.

"As a matter of fact it was an act of oblation to the only thing worth having on islands," said Carrol with an oblique glance at Sadie.

"I shall put it up in the cave with our matches," said Gibble.

The cave was a narrow fissure half-way up the head-land about eight feet deep into which it was possible to crawl. Gibble had found it in searching for a damp-proof place to keep the matches, after wrapping the box in many layers of dry bark. He stowed coconut fibre there too, with a notion of experimenting later in bed making.

"That reminds me," he said. "I was talking about it to Sadie; about making cloth from bark. Have you any idea how it's done?"

"No I haven't, though I've seen it done."

"You've *seen* it done?"

"Yes, on a film. All I remember about it is that some of the girls had nice breasts. I've got a notion that they whacked the bark with pieces of flat wood."

"What a pity you didn't make a careful note of it."

"Good lord, Gibby, what madhouse could have suggested that I'd ever need to make bark clothes. It it comes to that, what do any of us know about any special utility?   We are a magnificent example of the fact that civilization exists by the activities of a few specialists.   Take them out of the mass of mankind and it would go back to savagery in one generation."

"But that is the very thing; we must not allow ourselves to revert to—to—to—I mean, clothes, for instance.   We must have clothes of some sort.   These we have won't last for ever."

Sadie had mislaid her angry face for quite a long time, but now she suddenly found it.

"Forever!   Detestable words.   Of course, we'll get away from here before we need bark clothes.   Drivel, bark clothes.   I won't discuss such preposterous rot. Instead of sitting about talking idiocy, why don't you make something to signal at ships with?   You haven't attempted to——"

Carrol interposed hastily on a rising storm.

"Yes, yes, that's all right, Sadie, but while we *are* here we may as well fool about with anything that helps to fill in time.   I agree with Gibby; by all means have a shot at making some sort of material, if it's only something to sleep on.   And there's that hut.   You'll be dashed glad to have a decent shelter if it rains."

"Oh, I've no objection to *that*, and I've said all along that I'm sick of sleeping in grass seeds."

"Yes, yes, we'll set about that hut without fail tomorrow," said Gibble, with a glance at Carrol. . . .

And hut building, as both a utility and a diplomacy, was greatly facilitated by Pat's aptitude for the captions

of good fellowship.   Said Gibble to him next day, with
the back-pat of one worthy being to another:

"Now, Pat, I depend on you."

"And a man, Gibby lad, am I to be depended on."

"We will need, Pat, to begin by pulling down a number of boughs."

"Show me, Gibby, the boughs is needed pullin'."

"I have marked some, Pat, in that group of banyans
over behind the other beach.   We will try them first."

"We will try them, Gibby lad, and if they will not
do we will try them that will."

"We will, Pat, we will."

They went off with a fine show of zeal, and terms of
fulsome encouragement to labour receded inland.   Carrol came out of a lurking place in the scrub and joined
Sadie where she still lolled at the camp after the midday meal.

"Come on," he called.

"Come where?"

"Anywhere.   I've got to go for fruit, for one thing."

"Oh, bother tramping about that scrub."

"Well, come and find a place to sit about in."

"This is the best place for coolness; it's too hot in
there."

Carrol came over to take her hands.

"But those two will be back here soon and I've been
to a devil of a lot of trouble getting them both out of
the road together."

"Why?"

"You know why; so that I can have you alone to tell you how adorable you are."

He kissed her precisely on the brow, under the nostrils and on each ear.

"Now will you come?"

Sadie absently fondled his ear.

"No," she said.

"Be damned: you must."

He tugged at her arms, but was tugged into them by Sadie, who gave him a bear's hug and a bite, which invited a wrestling match, and Carrol's protests at indiscreet conduct in public. But she refused to leave the camp and Carrol had to slink off in a rage at last when Pat and Gibble were heard returning.

When he got back with his fruit they were stripping boughs and Sadie was excitedly discussing the site of her hut.

"I'll have it here between these two palms, with this hibiscus in front. That will shade it nicely and I'll see the flowers when I look out in the morning."

"We'll put a little fence round it and plant flowers in it and that will be your garden and all," said Pat.

"It wouldn't be a bad idea," said Sadie seriously.

No doubt the conception of a regenerated earth engaged them all, and house property is a universal passion. Even Carrol became interested in building the hut, in spite of Sadie's refusal to profit by it as a means of abstracting public attention from their private affairs. Her beach was now out of action as a reserve for wrestling matches, since he had given Gibble credentials to keep it under inspection, which Gibble did, quite unctuous with good conscience. He hasted for his fishing lines the moment Sadie went off to her beach. Carrol had to take interludes with her in private as chance designed. She found them pleasing, but refused to put herself out to make an entertainment of being wrestled with. She kept the business where it was, with a compact rejection of risks. Carrol tried having rows with her but that didn't work either. His temper was genuine enough, suspended on an exasperated lyricism, and he ranted at her with a fair vocabulary of abuse and some ingenuity for analysing feminine baseness, but Sadie only accepted such tributes to her self-esteem by inflating her prima donna's breast and saying disdainfully, "I never did think, Jimmy Carrol, that you were a gentleman."

But the really annoying thing was that she did not make a special distinction of Carrol's company from Gibble's, or for that matter, Pat's. She sat about the camp for hours watching her hut building when she could have been off with Carrol on the perfectly rational excuse of fruit getting. This could not be accounted to a policy of discretion, for she was incapable of intellectualizing a policy of action. By that trick she was able to maintain a complacent state of mind over their isolation, unless someone disturbed it by a maladroit emphasis on a very uncertain future. Pre-arrangements about life had to have a concrete inspiration before she allowed herself to indulge in proposals about them. Thus with the corner posts of her hut erected she was able to say concisely, "I will have my bed here, facing the door, and I must have a table here to put flowers on, and you must make a chair, and something to put my dress away in!"

Gibble found this very inspiring. He worked with an ardour that kept his face red-hot. Exposure to the sun was powerless to defeat its ready response to an accelerated blood pressure, but his beard had greatly improved it. He was astonished that he had not thought of growing a beard before, and acquired a secret passion for looking at it in waterholes. There, he was assured, was a resolute man. Sadie had also added an immense importance to the beard by giving her opinion that it suited him. Beards were a good deal discussed among them, chiefly because of Carrol's objection to his own. He suffered a temperamental aversion to hair on the face and was always speculating on devices for its removal, though he proved by experimental anguish that scraping it with a sharpened shell did not work. Nor was singeing with a hot coal effective, though they kept their hair short by burning the ends off; an operation performed with shouts of alarm and slapping at an ignited cranium.

But Gibble, besides pleasing himself with his beard, was now able to gratify a conception of himself as Sadie's chosen guardian. He blessed Carrol for having organized procedure on their affairs. To the distracting felicity of watching Sadie in the morning he now had the fine incitement to service of being watched by

her in the afternoon. The hut, as a topic of interest
to Sadie, allowed Gibble a share of her interest in it.
He acquired ease of converse with her. She went with
him gathering grasses for thatching. Once she vastly
exhilarated a conception of service by getting her petticoat tangled in a thorn bush, and calling imperiously
for him to release it.

"Be careful and don't tear it," she warned him, and
the nice operation of detaching a spiky spray that had

got between her legs gave Gibble's fingers such a series of shocks that their vibrations travelled via his backbone to his bare feet, and made his ears so hot that he felt them singeing. A thorn had scratched the inside of her thigh and she examined the wound so extensively under his eye that he was forced to turn his head away in alarm. Never had a leg appeared so large and so alive to him, for a convention that ends women's skirts at the knee does not really believe that there are legs also above it. He was still blushing when he came back to the camp, and his eye retained its consciousness of having looked on a marvel, and he added a fresh tint to his ears by finding Carrol observing him with austere disapproval.

Carrol disapproved strongly. If these intimacies were only any woman's trick of putting her price up all would have been well, but they were clearly nothing but that rank stupidity of Sadie's that failed to distinguish a bright entertaining fellow like himself from a bumbling bore of a parson like Gibble. When he pointed this out to Sadie she had the disgusting mendacity to say, "I regard Gibby as a thorough gentleman," and left Carrol grinding his teeth on expletives.

Pat also assumed a pose of zeal infected by Gibble's ideal of service, and encouraged their mutual labours in terms of offensive heartiness, especially when Carrol was about.

"Cock your eye at that, Gibby lad, and say is it straight."

"Higher to the right, Pat."

"Higher to the right it is, Gibby."

"Right, Pat."

"Right, Gibby."

"Mark your end, Pat."

"Marked it is, Gibby. And right it is, Gibby. And us is the boys to show not tools but brains is needed in house buildin'. Come along now, Jimmy boy, and put your heart into pullin' the ends off them branches."

Carrol usually cleared off into the scrub after a surfeit of optimism in those terms. It was quite unbearable on top of the stultifications imposed by Sadie, which brought the curse of their freed imagery into being. . . .

All very well the theory that Art is the antidote to its own emotional poison. Like any other dope, it generates a need greater than its power to satisfy. That, of course, is its job. But cut off the supply and the patient is hurled back on the mass of its petrified imagery which only booze and the solace of male talk can revitalize.

"Talk!" muttered Carrol. "The only exchange for it here is complete silence. Damme, a bit more of this and I'll go and live by myself on the other side of the island."

But he compromised on a dream of isolation by seeking out a hermitage on a barren promontory beyond Sadie's beach which was never used by them because only crude shrubs grew there and no fruit-bearing trees. A slab of rock had fallen across a narrow crevasse, roofing it, and Carrol cleared it of refuse and bedded it with bracken. In bad hours he made a moral bolt-hole of it, crawling into it with the frank relief of going into hiding. It generated in him the corruption of the coward; a theory of safety.

CHAPTER TEN.

I T WAS very hot; a stagnant dripping heat that hung motionless over the island and drained all virtue out of the air. It tasted turgid and warm against the gullet like the whiff of a stokehold.

Carrol had gone for fruit but gave it up; exertion in the scrub was impossible. The beaches were bad enough, but there was an illusion of space to breathe in there and he reached the small beach to flop down under a tree and drain.

Sadie was sprawled in the shade higher up, with an arm across her eyes, motionless, and it was some time before Carrol noticed her. He rose gaping, to move up and drop down beside her. She opened her eyes languidly a moment under her arm and closed them again, too inert for greeting.

"Lord! This heat——"

Carrol doddered a moment and let the objection go; identifying discomfort with the heat only intensified a perception of it. For an interval he sat quite vacuous, and then rolled over to let lassitude do what it pleased with him.

127

Sadie drowsed; she had that much control over her tissues, but Carrol was the type that cannot sleep by daylight. Either his mind or his feet insisted on keeping awake and demanding some sort of relief from boredom.

Sadie's hand lay beside him, limp and helpless, and he lifted it across his lips, inhaling its sweet aroma of health and youth. It stirred him to tender and remote thoughts about her, but not desire. With care, he smoothed the hair from her neck and slid an arm under it. She turned a little, settling herself against him. Their knees interlaced and their bodies supported a pose of rest.

Rest!

The heat ceased to be intolerable. By that subtle stimulus one body draws from another it became a narcotic. For a long time they lay motionless and contented in the happiest of all states, waking unconsciousness. But no state of felicity could do for Carrol without consciousness, and he kept closing his eyes against the filtered gold above to open them on Sadie's face. Laxity of all emotion had smoothed away its compressions; the pouted lips were open, the tinted eyelids closed; her breath touched his cheek like a gently moving fan.

"Damn love; I only want peace," thought Carrol, and he murmured into her lips, "I don't want you, Sadie, I only want to lie in your arms and not want you."

Sadie's lips made a childish sound that rejected talk,

and her arm round Carrol tightened and relaxed. There was a message there which brought Carrol's senses awake again and he kissed her. Her lips made no response; in fact, she was asleep again. But was she? That gentle pressure of her arm tightened and relaxed, like her even breathing. A caress—a command.

Of course! The body never makes a mistake in logic; only a fool fails to read its message. Carrol was not a fool.

Sadie's eyes opened slowly under his, amazed and happy. On that instant she was a catapult of rage, tossing him aside with arms of steel.

"Leave me alone! I hate you!"

Bitterly outraged, Carrol lay and glared at her. Contempt for such an anticlimax throttled him. Without a word he got up and went off into the scrub, rejecting her for ever.

He came out on the other beach to find the hut builders surrendered to the heat, lying in the shade with piles of boughs about them. Carrol threw himself down too, smothering his anger under arms thrown over his face. The others did not regard him, vacuous under physical discomfort that renounced exertion. Gibble humped his shoulders, giving a spasmodic twist at intervals. That unfortunate blood pressure of his felt the heat acutely. But he had resources of optimism denied the others and rose at last, stretching and gaping.

"Time we made a move, Pat."

"Time enough, Gibby."

Gibble went over to potter at the hut, now a gable

securely lashed with fibre and twisted grasses, on which the rafters were being completed. Pat turned on his elbow to survey at leisure Carrol's pose of complete dejection.

"And how's your affair with Lady Sadie goin'?" he asked conversationally.

Carrol opened his eyes to stare vacantly at him.

"Have you got her by this or are you on the job still?"

"Don't be a fool."

Carrol woke up to an investigation that must be disposed of as an unwarranted irrelevance, but Pat only grinned at him.

"Go on, now, haven't I seen through your joke of pushin' me off on Gibby to have her away to yourself?"

"Rot! You've seen more of her than I have these days."

"I haven't been bitin' the neck of her on the beach over yonder and that's where the difference comes in. Don't put yourself to the trouble of givin' me the lie, for I watched you myself from under a bit of a bush."

"You damned old snooper!"

The duplicities of their special grouping had to shift ground at that.

"You never saw much, anyhow. She's a bitch; I was a fool to put a hand on her. You needn't kid yourself on that score, Pat. I know her type; she's the sort of girl you go out with once and take damn good care not to again. I don't want her, anyway; be damned to her."

"Never say you'll let her beat you, now."

"She has."

"Not her. She's the sort would be eatin' you when not beatin' you. It's takin' her on the wrong side of her fancy you must be."

"She hasn't got a fancy in her damned head."

"Well, well, I'll be disappointed in you unless you make her see the light of reason, one way or another."

This was handsome, but Gibble's return deferred spiritual encouragement on that subject, and Carrol's frown warned Pat to shut up.

"This heat is really very trying," said Gibble, sitting down exhaustedly. "Quite impossible to work. I wish we could get a change."

"We'll get it soon, with luck," said Pat.

"Yes. At the same time we ought to have some sort of roof on the hut. Suppose it rains."

"Let it," said Carrol. "I wish it would rain enough to wash the bally island into the ocean."

"Yes, but—if we only piled all this green stuff on the rafters it would make some shelter."

"Oh, be damned; what's the good of bothering?"

Gibble rasped at his shoulders, red with prickly heat. His mind was troubled by a misgiving of laxity to an ideal of service, but he was glad, too, that the others rejected work.

Sadie came round from her beach, toiling across the sand with loathing. Her other face was set at its angriest glare that rejected a superheated universe of fools. Carrol glared too. An exchange of glances spat detestation at each other. Gibble cast a quick glance between them, alarmed by a revelation that he failed to comprehend. Sadie passed on to thrust her way viciously into the bush, leaving a suspended exposure behind her.

"And it's my opinion women is at the bottom of all our troubles too," said Pat.

"Who the hell's talking about women?"

Carrol's scowl at Pat exhibited less discretion than it demanded.

"Me, of course,' said Pat innocently. "I was thinkin' only this minute I wouldn't be here but for a slip of a wench in Sydney was walkin' out with Billy Powle that stoked with me on the *Monkseaton* seven year ago. I run agen him by chance in Liverpool Street, and this wench is with him at the time, a little dressed-up slim-dilly with a face like a baby's bottom for innocence. The three of us got celebratin' our meetin' in a pub up Surrey Hills way, for Billy and me had been like a pair of brothers, and lost sight of each other through me bein' run in at Baltimore and missin' the ship, and never sightin' one another till that minnit. He has a good job in the sewerage has Billy and is goin' to be married that day week, and give up booze for good, havin', as he said, the best girl in the world for his wife. He was wrong there in my opinion, for I had her away from him meself be the time he is snorin' on the pub sofa, and bought her from the feet up for the price of a hat she had a fancy for in a shop winder. I had a pocketful of cash and while

it lasted I had her too. But what use was it talkin'
reason to Billy when by this and that he come slinkin'
after us into a short-time house I am havin' her at, and
knocked all the pictures off the wall he did, and broke
a wash-stand before the people was there threw us out.
It's by bein' hurt in the feelin' at the things he says to
me more than by havin' no money left that I come to
sign on for the return run to Frisco that's landed me
where I am. I'd be workin' alongside Billy in the
sewerage this minnit but for that slip of a bitch comin'
between the pair of us."

"Which puts you out of the picture for coming between Billy and his bitch, of course."

"Of course, isn't that the trick they puts on us to
make us think we are doin' the whole thing ourselves?"

Gibble rose, always ill at ease under reminiscence
from Pat. He drifted to the edge of the scrub, listening at it with an expression of perturbation.

"It's got him too," said Pat.

"What has?"

"The buzz that's goin' on under your own nut this
minnit."

"Oh, it doesn't bother me. As for that goat, he's a
noble-minded parson, scared stiff over the whole
business."

"He's not so scared to be cockin' an eye at her over
yonder skippin' out in her skin, makin' beknowns he's
not there watchin' her at all."

"You seem to make a business of keeping this dam'
beach under observation, blast you."

"What else is there to do on it?   I was given an eye in me head to make use of, and little enough usin' it gets here."

He stretched to look out across the reef and add: "The sea yonder is gettin' a roll up from under, and that means a push of wind from somewhere.   Let it come and welcome and blow the cobwebs off this place."

The sun sank that evening a crude magenta ball behind a bank of liver-coloured cloud, and turned a sea of molten bronze to lead.   At intervals a wave rose in the sullen mass and ran out to sea, to sink in a floating line of foam.   Night shut down on them as if the island had slid into a vast oven, and the backwash of moving waters broke insistently at the reef.

Sadie came to the evening meal subdued.   Her temper had gone in an interval alone with the oppressive forces of nature, and she kept glancing out to sea, or overhead with little impatient movements of the shoulders.   Pat ate largely, but the others palpably took their food down as people in an emergency, not wanting it, but feeling they may need it.

While the light lasted, Gibble had them pile greenstuff on the rafters, and vastly eased his own mind. He was busy for a time carrying in brushwood before coming back to the fire.

"It's fairly rain-proof, I think," said he.   "If it rains, and I think it will rain, we'll all go into it.   You don't mind?" he added to Sadie.

"Prefer it," said Sadie abruptly.   She shivered, confessing her uneasiness at a suspended threat of violence

in the still thick air.   Carrol's bad temper left him in
a desire to soothe her alarm.

"It's nothing to bother about, Sadie, only a storm
of sorts coming," he said.

"I hate storms."

"But we have the hut, you know, quite an adequate
shelter," said Gibble.   "There's really no cause for
alarm."

"None at all but a bit of a blow will do us all the
world of good," said Pat heartily.

He turned into his lair, assured of ease in a concrete
earth.   Carrol caught Sadie's eye behind Gibble's back
to nod at the beach with raised eyebrows and a wink;
a compacted message which read, "Don't worry, meet
me out there later."

Sadie shuddered at the dark void and turned a frown-
ing question back at Carrol, which he disposed of with
a reassuring smile.   "Take my tip and turn in, Sadie,"
he said.

"Do," urged Gibble.   "There's really nothing to
fear."

"I suppose there's nothing else to do," said Sadie,
and went, with a doubtful glance back at Carrol.

Carrol retired too, as a hint to discourage Gibble from
staying up any longer.   But Gibble stayed up, pottering over odd jobs.   He cleaned the day's catch of fish
and hung them by the gills from a twig.   Then he put
in another nuisance of an interval building a shelter of
rocks over the fire to keep the embers from getting wet.
But at last there was nothing more to do, and with a

doubtful inspection of the camp he crawled into his lair too.

Carrol let the fire dim to a faint glow before creeping cautiously from his couch and thence across the sand by a course that brought Sadie's shelter between him and the camp. With a breathed note of caution he reached a hand in to touch Sadie, and she came swiftly out to him, and clung to him with relief. Softly they drew off till the broken ground of the headland was reached and Carrol helped Sadie to a seat beside him.

"That's better; it was oppressive up there at the camp for some reason," he said.

"Horrible!"

She twined her arms tightly round him, pressing her face to his neck. He could feel little shivers run through her tense body.

"Why, what's the matter, Sadie?"

"I'm frightened."

"But there's nothing to be frightened of. Your nerves have gone with the heat, that's all."

"I suppose so. . . ."

She relaxed a little and opened her eyes at the void about them. "But I hate this waiting—and this darkness. It seems close to us."

Carrol soothed her, running caressing fingers about her cheek and smoothing her satin shoulders with his arm. But he glanced furtively around and aloft, oppressed by the sense of inertia threatened by an approaching force. Nothing broke the deadly stillness but the sudden rush of a wave out there, driven by a mysterious power within itself. A sibilance, faint and stealthy, reached him from the unseen palms, and a ghostly shudder passed through the undergrowth. Far away he seemed to hear a faint moaning.

"It's coming," he thought, and tugged Sadie up. "We'd better get back to the camp, or perhaps under the banyans; curse this darkness. . . ."

They stood there foolishly embraced, muddled by a conviction of nowhere to go. A gust of wind scurried across the treetops and that distant moan drew out to a long-sustained whine, like a vast dynamo speeding towards them, whose note surged to a roar as it struck the island. . . .

Carrol and Sadie were blown flat and held there as by solid matter in transit, backed by irresistible forces. Flying sand whipped their faces and the air was a mass of spray and hurtling greenstuff. They clung to each other with closed eyes and coherence beaten out of them. A bedlamite uproar confounded all impulses but those which gripped to hold fast a human body. To be alone was the last terror. . . .

It was not by any sensate proposal that they crawled at last to the lee of a rock and there crouched to recover the breath driven from their lungs. Carrol was trying to shout at Sadie, "The banyans—roots—banyans—" while Sadie was tugging furiously at him and screaming something that the wind whipped from her mouth. Then he caught it—"The cave."

To be sure, the cave. But in that flying blackness movement was like falling into a void of nightmare. Carrol peered beneath his arm to sense the mass of the headland against a dim burst of seas beyond, but Sadie carried a better sense of locality than he did and screamed at him to come. They had to crawl gripped together, using their combined weight to hold down a resistance against the wind, but they reached the overhanging ledge of rock that sheltered the cave's entrance.

Crawling into that windless little heaven was such a shock of relief that they both collapsed together, helpless with gratitude. The rock ledge drove the wind sheer overhead and left them secure in a vacuum. Narrowed by the cave's entrance, the sound of a universe gone mad reached them in one unchanging boom.

The compulsion of terror still possessed Sadie's muscles and she held Carrol so tightly that he was forced to release the grip of her fingers. With that she gave up all to a blessed sense of security and went limp all over. Carrol lay awhile to let rationality return to his thoughts with a long sigh of thanksgiving.

"Hell! that *was* wind. I never knew there was such a thing before."

He sat up cautiously in the dead blackness of the cave and felt for their positions. The floor was thick with fibre collected by Gibble, and at that Carrol uttered a sound of consternation.

"God! Sadie!"

Sadie, still inert, did not answer and he shook her.

"Sadie! the others!"

Sadie stirred and asked vaguely, "What others?"

"Pat and Gibby."

A questioning silence between them in the dark was broken uneasily by Carrol.

"They ought to be up here with us. Damnation, we can't leave them out there. I wonder if I could get back to them."

Sadie's arms came out of the dark to clutch him.

"Impossible! How could you? And besides——"

"But hell! consider that beach——"

"What good could you do, getting blown to pieces too? You mustn't go. Madness!"

"But hang it——"

"Don't you dare leave me."

She tugged him into her arms, making sure of him. Carrol muttered protests, not sincere, and a little pumped-up optimism. "Perhaps they're all right—the bush would break half the force of that wind—we got the worst of it, out in the open. . . ."

Sadie's impatient lips found his in the dark and sealed them against the utterance of imbecilities. Carrol suddenly forgot to utter them. He forgot Pat and Gibble, forgot himself, forgot everything on earth but Sadie. · That corruption of the coward in him tried to formulate a theory of discretion but he forgot the fatuous impulse too. . . .

Quite another tempest was released in that little cave, blowing all resistance to it flat.

Outside, a shrieking barrier of wind sealed them against a world gone mad with the turmoil of riven clouds and driven seas, streaming away into the night its hoot of derision for a rational earth. . . .

CHAPTER ELEVEN

CARROL woke to a novel sense of padded
warmth against his eyelids and shifted his face
to discover it pillowed against Sadie's throat.
In the filtered grey of dawn he reviewed with astonishment her face inclined to his, asleep with a divine
composure. The heavy lips and eyelids were calm with
disdain for trivial disruptions begotten by men and
hurricanes, under the rise and fall of those undaunted
breasts of hers she breathed with noiseless ease.

144

Her mask was lovely to Carrol and he kissed it with honeymoon ardour, awakening Sadie to discover him with vague and puzzled eyes. Straightway she wound her arms round him and closed her eyes again, refusing to forego the rewards of sleep.

But Carrol was wide awake now and very much aware of a theory of benevolence designed to go wrong.

"Lord! Sadie, those precautions we didn't take!"

Sadie only shook him with closed eyes and pulled him closer.

"But listen, Sadie——"

She refused to listen and for a honeymoon interval Carrol forgot to talk. From that he was shocked back to recall another overlooked trifle.

"God! Pat and Gibby!"

That brought them both wide awake, staring an alarmed question, which made them reluctant to move for more reasons than a disturbed moment of lyricism.

"This won't do, Sadie, we'll have to get out and see what's happened.—I suppose they're all right but—but listen! Whatever happens, you spent the night up here alone. Say you couldn't sleep and walked along the beach for coolness and managed to get up here when the storm hit us. . . ."

Sadie nodded and Carrol kissed her. They crawled to the mouth of the cave and looked forth. It still blew a strong gale and they stared astonished at the turmoil of seas racing mad-capped to the horizon, and the incessant boom and explosion of spray along the reef. A head of rock cut off their view of the beach, but a section below them was disturbingly littered with a riff-raff of greenstuff.

"Phew!" said Carrol. "Wait here till I get off over the headland; I'll turn up from the other end of the beach."

He crawled along the rock bastion below the cave and vanished over a slide of rubble leading to the other beach.

Sadie came doubtfully forth, drawing up her shoulders at a fresh sharpness in the air. At the sight of the beach she paused again, amazed at its disorder of wrecked branches and fallen trees and the masses of sand blown against everything. There was no sign of movement at the camp and that alarmed her. And then there was a decrepit figure that limped out of the debris, supporting itself on a stick. It was Gibble, and he did not look up, but peered into the wreckage with a strained and fearful air.

"Gibby!" called Sadie and waved to him.

Gibble staggered, stared, and was transfixed. The sun shone briefly from a wrack of hurrying clouds and into that morning glory walked Sadie, beautiful as a release from fear.

"My God! I thought you were lost. I thought——"

Gibble's foot and his nerves collapsed together and he slumped down on his knees, weeping. Sadie hastened to him, charmed to console torments in her service. She patted his shoulder, bending over him.

"Poor old Gibby; it's all right; I'm quite safe. I slept in the cave all night."

"The cave!"

Gibble blinked at her, recovered from tears. "The cave. I never once thought of the cave."

From a bemused moment another alarm returned. "Carrol! Was he—what's become of him?"

"I don't know; isn't he with you?"

"No, I haven't seen him since last night. I thought——"

He stared at her, fumbling with his lips.

"I couldn't sleep and went along the beach for coolness and just managed to reach the cave when the storm came," explained Sadie.

"Thank God you did; it was frightful here. Pat's hurt too."

"Are you?"

"Yes, I've sprained my ankle. I ran out and fell over something; a tree. And then I was blown flat. An awful night. I managed to crawl into the bush against a tree. I was terrified, wondering what had become of you."

"Poor Gibby. But your foot is swollen. Give me your arm."

She helped him up; an astonishing benediction of her bare arm under his. It bewildered other concepts than help to a sprained ankle. Staggering between Sadie and his crutch, another accent of astonishment was jerked out of Gibble.

"Carrol! There's Carrol!"

Carrol had emerged from the scrub higher up and was staring about him. They waved and he came hurrying but at the camp stopped, stared, and turned inwards. When they arrived he was bending over Pat, who sat with a peculiar twist in his neck while Carrol examined his back with comments of alarm.

"What a mess! Good God! how did it happen?"

"A tree fell on me," said Pat.

"Hell!" protested Carrol.

The skin of Pat's back was badly rasped from shoulder to thigh and the blood had clotted on it, drawing a horrified protest from Sadie too, as she bent to examine it.

"Go on now, it's no more than a bit of a scrape that grazed me in passin'," said Pat, highly pleased with the drama of his lacerations. "The worst is a crack I come by somehow in the neck, and another in the leg here is that stiff I can't bend it with aise."

"I don't wonder; it's bruised black. But we must do something about that back. Can you spare a bit of that shirt of mine, Sadie?"

"Yes, if it's still there. And Gibby's sprained his ankle," she added, backing into the scrub.

"Hell!" said Carrol, giving this new disaster its tribute of concern.

"Yes, it's rather badly swollen," said Gibble with pride. "I ran out and fell over a tree. After that I was helpless. Just managed to crawl to a tree and stay there. Didn't know what had happened to anyone. An awful night."

"Well, I had luck," said Carrol. "A sense of something wrong roused me just before the storm struck us

and I went along the beach. I was close to those big
banyans and crawled between the roots. But how did
Sadie get through?"

"She got up to the cave," said Gibble with animation. "Extraordinary! Just as the storm——"

"I've found the shirt," said Sadie, returning. "Lucky
I had it stowed away in the log. Shall I help?"

"Yes, hold some water for me."

They washed the injured back, to Pat's amusement
at concern for what he called a bit of a scrape. It was
a bad surface laceration, but not so bad when cleaned
of blood and presented in order for healing. "We
can't tie it up, there isn't enough linen," said Carrol.
"It will heal better exposed to the air but you'll have
to sleep on your face."

"Bother doctor's orders and look after Gibby there
with his bunged foot."

Gibble's ankle was bathed and bandaged and couches
prepared for the invalids, who reposed strangely aware
of worth, as if by a voluntary heroism they had taken
the community's disasters on themselves.

"And now, food," said Carrol, raking up his hair at
the disorder of the camp.

"The fire's out," said Gibble. "We'll have to use
another match. There ought to be some fish somewhere; I cleaned them last night. And plantains—
there was a stock of them too. . . ."

The food was recovered and for an interval Sadie
and Carrol were busy. A consciousness of benevolent
zeal emanated from them, very gratifying to the self-

esteem of all. With the fire burning briskly and a mess of grilled fish and roast plantains smoking hot on platters of bark even a lacerated back and a sprained ankle could account themselves a fresh exhilaration to the adventure of life, with its background of wild seas and spouting reefs, and flashes of sunlight dramatizing the wrecked beach.

"And that reminds me you owe me a fiver if ever we come in sight of a pub agen," said Pat to Carrol.

"It shall be paid. Meanwhile you'll have to take luck's reward in a phantom booze-up."

"I have a feelin' on me I've had one," said Pat, eating fish at an acute angle to his stiff neck.

"The thing that strikes me as wonderful is that Sadie should have been near the cave when the storm broke," said Gibble. "It was more than providential. I am convinced—convinced—that she was guided there."

"H'm—er—yes," said Carrol. "Possibly you are right; I wouldn't be surprised if you were. In fact, Gibby, I was only thinking this morning that there's quite a lot in that theory of benevolence of yours, quite a lot. It makes things go wrong only to put them right in the most unexpected way."

Sadie was busy with a fish and merely raised those brilliant eyebrows at it for a moment.

CHAPTER TWELVE

PEACE returned to the island. The sun passed over a serene sky with mild cumuli at the horizon. Light trade winds ruffled the palmtops at evening. Only the sea still ran a giant swell that picked out the reef in a display of brilliant fountains.

Carrol surveyed his morning exertions at the camp, with the injured disposed for the day on their piles of brushwood.

"Your back would skin over better if you wouldn't keep turning over when asleep and opening it up," he told Pat.

"It's in hospital we are with the doctor makin' his rounds. I was hospital orderly in India an' many's the round I made with him. The back's none so bad—it's this leg is the trouble goin' so stiff on me. I never knowed a bit of a bruise to be so bothersome."

"It's a wonder your leg wasn't broken."

"Haven't I told you I'm the luckiest man ever walked?"

"You have, several times. All the same I wouldn't stretch such magnificent luck too far; you might get hurt some day."

"I'd be hurt an' welcome for a bit of fun to end comin' out of hospital with."

"The fact is we'll have to build against another bust-up of that sort," said Carrol to Gibble.

"The hut stood, you see."

"Yes, but it offered little resistance to the wind. I wouldn't trust it with a roof on."

"That storm must have been exceptional. Consider the beach when we came here and look at it now. If storms like that were common the place would have been littered with timber."

"All the same, I wouldn't bank on a system of benevolence that loses its head on those terms."

He glanced at the reef, where Sadie had been fishing, but she had gone beyond the headland.

"Time I was off for fruit," he said, and turned into the scrub. When he came out again on the other beach Sadie was loitering there with two small fish strung on a reed.

"What a time you've been," she complained.

"Household duties detained me." He twined an arm round her and they loitered on, free of the island.

"Let me see, will we go for fruit first or——"

"Pooh to fruit."

"Pooh to fish too, I suppose.   You have a rotten catch there."

"I can't be fishing all day."

"We must eat, as well as be discreet.   I suspect our absence will be noticed if we spend so much time getting fruit.   We were all yesterday afternoon getting a small supply of guavas. . . ."

They were at least two hours not getting fruit that morning before Carrol got an acute attack of discretion and sped off to the nearest fruit trees and Sadie returned humming to her fishing at the reef. . . .

For two hours Gibble's eyes had hardly left the headland watching for her return.   Of course, she might be fishing round the bend, but she had left the beach swinging two small fish and she now returned with two small fish.   Perhaps the fish were not biting but there was Carrol still away fruit getting and there was plenty of fruit on the island and millions of fish in its water.

All day Gibble was forced to speculate for and against duplicity in those absences of Carrol and Sadie, from which they always returned separately.   If Gibble was to accept the fair seeming of such a return, why had nothing followed his own declaration of devotion for Sadie?   He had wept with relief at her safety from the storm and she had patted his shoulders and helped him up with her bare arm, and sealed off an impression of herself that tingled up to Gibble's armpit every time he thought of it.   That event had rushed life to a crescendo for Gibble and there stopped, and he was incessantly aware of its stultified arrest.   Something should have happened on a mutual confession of tenderness: something *must* happen. . . .

Nothing happened. And a rotten job that leaves you, intellectualizing a procedure for love which you are incompetent to practise. If Sadie would only lift her eyelids to give him the cue for action, Gibble had his few well-chosen words ready for her. He practised choosing such words constantly, and supplied Sadie's answers to them; a phantom converse of great delicacy which was crudely intruded on all day by Pat, who insisted on talking to mitigate the boredom of convalescence. Escape by crutches was not permitted.

"Will you stop your hoppin' about like an old fowl and listen to me a minute," he would command. . . .

That was another affliction to words not uttered. Gibble failed to denounce an autobiographical passion that used war and toil as a stage setting for a grand reality of beatings and boozings and drabbings in all the ports of earth. An awful compulsion to the treachery of ears, listening to such things. Gibble was not aware that he went through life in terror of his ears. They were always threatening to confound the things that should not be known with the things he must not know. All faith is a conscientious practice of deafness, and how could he practise it hobbled by a sprained ankle to a chant of reminiscence that acclaimed debauch the choice reward of a full life? When Carrol was about the camp Gibble was able to fub off a perverted act of listening on him, but alone with Pat inattention was not allowed. Pat was a talker who demanded a listener's eye as well as his ears.

At the same time, Carrol's presence at the camp when Sadie was also there brought other alarms to Gibble's ears that he failed to account for. Perhaps it was the way their voices dropped a tone when speaking together even about trivialities; no policy of discretion learns to conquer that trick. . . .

In that covert inspection of those two, Gibble was damnably troubled by Sadie's eyelids. He watched them more for admissions to Carrol than for concessions to himself, but got neither. And jealousy *must* know the worst. It was the same annoyance that Carrol had been subjected to over her refusal to state a preference between Gibble's company and his own.

But Sadie's eyelids refused to make a fuss over any other affairs but their own, and when a disturbance clicked them open starings made no distinction of Gibble's identity from Pat's or Carrol's. It was very baffling, for without a little indulgence in the optics of tenderness how was he to get at those few well-chosen words, and handicapped at that by hopping after her on one leg?

Then there was the discovery of the boat. . . .

She had sunk at the reef where it was deepest and diving too dangerous because of the branching masses of coral. The commotion of the storm had set up such a backwash at the reef that the boat had been shifted from its submerged rocks to the sand bottom of the lagoon. It lay clearly defined in the pellucid morning depths, and Carrol's shouts brought Gibble hopping on his crutch from the camp.

"What is it?" he called.

"The boat."

"What, can you see her?" cried Gibble excitedly.

"Yes, it's her all right."

Carrol dived, to reappear blowing, and dive again. . . .

"It's deeper than it looks," he said, puffing over a third effort to reach the boat, and with that sent a shout across the water for Sadie, who came out on the flat rocks from her beach to call, "What's the matter?"

"The boat!   Come on, you dive better than I do."

Sadie plunged in and swam to him, putting her face under water to peer below.

"It's not so deep," she said, preparing to dive.

"The hatchet," called Gibble.   "It's stuck in the thwarts; I put it there myself."

With a flick of long legs Sadie vanished and Carrol shot down after her, leaving Gibble disturbed at a naked vanishing in the depths.   Carrol was first back and Sadie popped up a second later.

"I got down to it all right," she told Carrol.   "Race you this time to see who gets the hatchet."

They dived together with a licentious flirting of legs at the sky and bobbed up together in a conflict of splashes.

"You bumped me, Jimmy Carrol," cried Sadie indignantly.   "You take the other end this time."

"Wait a minute, blast it," puffed Carrol.

"Pooh!" said Sadie, and dived again, leaving Carrol to peer down at her from the surface. He could see her long figure sprawling over the boat with frog-like kickings, and a moment later she shot to the surface, waving the hatchet. All shouted, and woke Pat from a morning doze at the camp.

"What in the name of Jasus ails the lot of you?" he called, peering from the shade.

"The hatchet! we've got it," shouted Gibble.

He forgot his lame leg and those two hastening from the water, and bumped down on the sand to have the hatchet handed to him for an ecstatic handling of good honest iron.

"Wonderful—wonderful!" he kept repeating.

Then he was aware of something a little more wonderful still, and that was Sadie standing beside him as naked as Venus. His eyes shot back to the hatchet like retractile bodies responsive to shock, but that did not mitigate the confounding knowledge that Carrol was standing there also as naked as Sadie, and that they were talking together as if they had clothes on.

"We might get the biscuit tins too, if they aren't fixed down. I think they were," Carrol was saying.

"It wouldn't take much to shift the boat if we only had a line."

"The boat's no use but there's the other hatchet and the water breaker. There was a can of oil too, I think, and a grappling iron; not that they'd be much use. . . ."

They scampered back to the water, leaving Gibble bemused at treasure retrieved at the cost of shock to a

repressed retina.   He sat there fingering the hatchet
with a most disturbed perception of those two naked
bodies bobbing about in the water, and vanishing into
it between gusts of talk.   They got up the water breaker
and the grappling iron but failed to find the other
hatchet.   Then he was aware of them at the surface
with something else ravished from the sea and scrambled up, signalling agitatedly.

"It's a two quart bottle," called Carrol.   "Eh, what?"

"Hide it," Gibble was saying in a keyed-down voice.
"What?"

Gibble glanced back at the camp and signalled them
closer and they swam in with the bottle between them.

"Don't let Pat see that," said Gibble anxiously.   "It's
got spirits of some sort in it."

"Spirits?   How did it get there?"

"It was there all the while.   Take it away and hide
it."

"You'd better take it round to your beach, Sadie,"
said Carrol.   She nodded and went off, trailing the
bottle below the surface.   Carrol and Gibble looked
round at Pat, who was craning at them from the camp.

"What is it you have now?" he called.

"Nothing; we can't find the other hatchet."

"I suppose it was the regulation boat's supply," said
Gibble in a low voice.   "I kept it dark from Pat in the
boat, knowing he'd never rest till he'd drunk it.   He
mustn't know we've got it."

"No, it would only exasperate the desire for more.

And we might need it ourselves, at a pinch. Well, that's all to be got from the boat by diving."

A relief to Gibble, with Sadie's return to the camp dressed and therefore to be looked at in the presence of others. Only when others looked at her nudity he found it intolerable. . . .

"Now we will build a stately pleasure house," said Carrol, going round clipping at trees with the hatchet. "The secret of bark clothes will also be investigated. . ."

In fact, he went off with the hatchet that afternoon to look for samples of bark, taking Sadie with him. Her opinion on fabrics was accounted necessary, and Gibble heard their voices recede in the woods with depression. It came into his mind that an ease of address very distinguished at church bazaars had suffered a repression on that island; a discovery that accounted for much. He glanced at Pat dozing after the midday meal, and rose cautiously to hobble away from the camp. He was sick of those interminable stories, and more sick of having their subject matter dictated by a stoker. Carrol had the same impertinent trick too. They both stated opinion on life freely but never invited it from him. The unspoken assumption was that he had nothing to say worth listening to. It was intentional; they depreciated him. . . .

He paused to listen at the undergrowth but heard nothing. They were well away in there, unreachable by a sprained ankle. Getting bark!

He forgot his injury at that, and retrieved it from the ground with a grimace of fury.

"Damnation!"

A trenchant outcry, which astonished him. "Damnation!" he repeated, but in a milder tone. It went well with the discovery that he had conceded too much to controversial insolence. He had allowed that stoker to talk as he pleased and Carrol to air offensive theories without protest. He began to contest them on the spot, and said some very effective things for which neither Carrol nor Pat could find a retort. He had to find retorts for them of such a feeble-minded nature that he was able to crush them both with withering rhetoric. The exercise heated him as much as hopping about in the sand and he sat down in the shade to continue it. At intervals the thread of contention lapsed while he listened at the scrub for voices. A damning silence in there, which goaded him to a fearful impatience. He was out of it; debarred from action; forced to posture as a dummy to that execrable Pat's stories, while Carrol . . .

It was quite unbearable and he scrambled up, hurt his foot, damned it and hobbled back to the camp before he had time to think of not doing it, and Pat was awake and annoyed at his desertion.

"This thinkin' of nothin' all day is like sittin' over a hole with the bottom knocked out of it. I have no likin' for it at all at all," said he; and added impatiently, "Sit down then. If it wasn't for makin' a noise at times we wouldn't know we was alive in this place."

But as Gibble stood there wobbling on his crutch Pat shouted at him, "Sit down I'm tellin' you," and Gibble sat down, vastly incensed with himself for doing so.

"That's better," said Pat, appeased. "A man must have company, no matter what. I mind once doin' a stretch of fourteen days in Baltimore, at a time I near had the shakes on me from a week's hard drinkin', and I walked that cell for hours, thinkin' I would die every two seconds from findin' it impossible to go on livin'. The liquor we had there was rotgut I will admit, but the horrors themselves is nothin' to bein' caught on the way to them, and havin' the beginnin' an' endin' of everything knocked from under you but the one thought of wishin' you could go mad on the spot for a relief to it. Have you ever had that feelin' on your mind?"

"No," said Gibble shortly.

"Of course, you haven't. You wouldn't be a parson if you had."

"What do you mean by that?" exclaimed Gibble.

"Sure no man would be a parson with the hot blood under his hat to be anything else. You'll admit that, I think," said Pat rationally.

Monstrous, to sit simmering in silence and find no words to rescue a vocation as one of the elect from the tolerent contempt of a stoker.

"For look at you there," went on Pat impartially, "Sittin' about all day like a burst bag of bran and a fine high-steppin' girl like Sadie waitin' for you to put the come-hither McGinnis on her."

"I won't have you talking about Sadie like that," exclaimed Gibble. A flush of anger accented all sorts of white dents about his lips and he was forced to capture a sensation of losing his breath by a resort to violence.

"I won't have it," he shouted.

"Now you're in a temper and that will do you good," said Pat complacently. "I'm not sayin' there mightn't be the makin's of a man somewhere in you, forbye you could get closer to a wench than hoppin' about at her from behind a rock."

"I——" stammered Gibble, and swallowed a large mental hot potato. He had the sensation of being accused of infamous practices, and what was more infamous still, felt he had really practised them. The grand illusion of invisibility on which the earth exists was suddenly demolished, leaving him exposed to the crude inspection of a stoker. That exposist, strange to say, seemed to have no sense of having functioned as a clinic of shameful revelations.

"Not but what she's well worth lookin' at whichever way you take her," said he. "Many's the squint I've given her meself, with her pretendin' there's no one about but the saygulls. A girl with a figure like that would never rest aisy unless someone was lookin' at it, and the marvel is you are such a ditherin' runt as to be creepin' under a rock instead of gallopin' out at her like a man with a bit of hot blood in him. It's to be hoped Jimmy there is makin' better use of his time."

Gibble tried not to hear that. Complicity with that

wretched Pat's antics of watching Sadie bathing was worse to bear than a conception that exposed him doing the same thing in private. He sat with a stultified eye on the horizon, as a point of space most removed from an intolerable intimacy at his elbow.

Pat twisted himself into a posture of comfort, satisfied with the release of talk.

"I will say it's not all luck that comes by women, all the same," said he. "I could prove that to you by a nigger that come aboard the *Maralia* at Algeciras, askin' to work his passage to Baltimore. The captain put him in the starboard watch—Captain Gratten his name was, and the best captain I ever sailed with, and a man I'd put me head in pawn for, to save comin' at trouble. And trouble he got that trip, for two days out from Gibraltar the starboard watch is all aft the main hatch swearin' they wouldn't have this nigger in the fo'castle, for the smallpox is broke out on him. I was below at the time, bein' in the port watch, and word is sent down for me to come up, for it's known I was hospital orderly in India could tell the signs of it on him.

" 'Plunket,' says Captain Gratten to me, 'just have a look at the nigger yonder and say if these hoodlums is right about him.'

"The nigger is sittin' by the forward winch, and be this an' that I have me suspicions what ailed him, but not to make him onaisy I give him a fill of tobacco.

" 'You're not lookin' too good on it,' I says.

" 'I'm all right,' says he.

" 'Are you?' says I, 'for I am one that has a touch of the ladies' fever on me this minute.' I hadn't, of course, but says that only to draw him. 'Is that so?' says he, and owns up what is troublin' him. 'Let's have a look at you and I'll get a dose or two will cure you,' says I.

"Begob, it's far gone he was. I goes back to the bridge and says I, 'Captain, it's not the smallpox that nigger has but the great pox and he's past curin'.'

" 'Be damned to him,' says Captain Gratten, 'for I'll be quarantined for him like as not, when we get to Baltimore, havin' no medical opinion, and he's not signed on, and I've no right to have him here at all,' he says.

" 'Don't trouble your head, Captain,' says I. 'He'll never see Baltimore.'

" 'You think so, Plunket?' says he.

" 'I'm sure of it,' says I.

"He gives me a look and takes a turn, rubbin' his bald head.

" 'And what's to be done with him the while, for the crew won't have him in the fo'castle?' says he.

" 'There's room for him in the starboard closet,' says I.

" 'I put him in your charge entirely, Plunket,' says he.

"You'll not believe me when I say not wan of them hounds of the starboard watch would give me a hand stowin' that nigger away in the closet, swearin' he was rotten, which was true enough. It's me has to feed him and give him his dose of jollop for the look of things, keepin' an eye on him betimes I'm smokin' a pipe between watches. Every mornin' Captain Gratten would say to me, 'And how's that canary of yours gettin' on, Plunket?'

" 'In my opinion he'll not last three days out of Baltimore Captain,' I'd say.

" 'You ought to know,' he'd say, 'havin' been hospital orderly in India.' "

Pat paused there, as inviting attention to the clarity and veracity of his narrative.

"It appears I was right," said he, "for on the very mornin' Captain Gratten says to me, 'We'll be off Baltimore Tuesday mornin', Plunket,' I says to him, 'Then I'll ask you for a bit of sail cloth and a lump of pig iron.'

"Wait now, I'm wrong. I has a look at the nigger to make sure all is over with him before askin' for the canvas to cover him up decent with. And sure I has him trimmed up as nice as you could wish your own corpse to be by the time we changed watches, and I calls out to the starboard watch was standin' off lookin' at me, 'Two of yous will bear a hand to dump him,' I says.

" 'None of us will,' says they.

" 'He's as dead as mutton,' says I.

" 'It's more than he was before you tied him up so neat,' says one.

"I give that one a thump knocked his head agen the winch chains."

" 'Is anyone here will dispute the opinion of me was hospital orderly in India that he's dead?' says I.

"None of them did, but for all that I has to lug him

out meself and upend him agen the side an' give him a toss by the heels sent him over as neat as could be."

Gibble's eyes detached themselves slowly from the skyline to give Pat a vacant stare.

"Wait now," said Pat. "I'm not to the end yet, though you'd think the thing was done with, bein' no more than a nigger was a nui snce to himself and everybody else aboard. By one thing and another the crew got talkin' ashore in Baltimore, and the first thing I know is bein' ordered to an inquiry was sittin' at the Marine Board as to how come this nigger aboard and by what means he come to die there. Begob, when I come into the court there is Captain Gratten has been examined, and is wipin' the sweat from his bald head, and gives me a look to speak up and put the matter right. An' put it right I did, of course, havin' been hospital orderly in India and knowin' the signs of them that dies of the pox, for which there was a medical man there to bear me out, and bein' able to say as well by the nigger tellin' me of it, 'twas Captain Gratten's kindness give him a free passage to Baltimore.

"The Captain and me come out of court together and when we are round the corner he gives a whistle to clear his breath and shakes me by the hand.

" 'It's the first easy minute I've had this day, Plunket,' he says, 'for by the grandest bit of luck there wasn't a tittle between what I told them and what you did.'

" 'And why not, Captain, seein' it was the simple truth?' says I.

" 'Of course, of course,' says he."

Gibble's eyes had remained fixed on Pat with the fascination of abhorrence. Now they were transferred swiftly back to the sea rim. His lips made the motions of speaking but did not.

"And that," said Pat comfortably, "was how I come by one of the best booze-ups I ever had, for Captain Gratten's sister kept a pub in Liverpool, our next port out from Baltimore, and he made me free of the bar for a month, he did—the best captain I ever sailed with."

But Gibble's eyes refused to leave the sea rim, beyond which lay that safe kind earth where one practised self-approval all day long before an audience buttressed millions deep against crude and lawless deeds—or against a greater evil still: a submerged memory begotten by them.

With the last long rays of the sun trailing shadows to the water's edge came Sadie and Carrol, loafing back round the headland, and bearing some very inadequate samples of bark for inspection.

"There you are and you and Pat can have a hell of a good time whacking them with bits of wood," said Carrol.

He gouged a coconut, drank, and composed himself on his couch, saying, "You can be cook tonight, Sadie, I'm too tired for housework after bark-hunting all the afternoon."

Sadie obediently made up the fire and began to clean fish. Gibble sat fingering the pieces of bark without looking at them. Pat got up to stretch, yawn, and experiment with his leg before sitting down again. For an interval all three stared vacantly at the placid sea, tinted purple in the last rays of the sun.

"There's too much sea about this place and that's one of the things is wrong with it," said Pat. "The best of stokin' is that between watch and watch it's dam' little you see of it at all. I'm tired to the guts with lookin' at it."

"Are you?" said Carrol. "I was just thinking it's one of the few things we don't get sick of because it never lets your eye rest. I'm beginning to love this eternal ring of sea round us. Why? I know why. Safety! That's the key word to islands. Here I'm safe from the bloody insane privilege of having to fight for a living on earth. If there isn't a hell of a joke behind that, Olympus doesn't know what a comic paper is. Safe from the Suburbs; safe from the Saved; safe from the stinking herd of wowsers and by-law mongering morons called human beings."

Gibble's stare came slowly round to look at him, as bemused as in its rejection of that other earth of violence and danger.

"And by ginger, there's another thing we're safe from here, and that's Art," said Carrol. "Curse music; I hope I never hear another note of it. I notice I'm beginning to learn the trick of dozing awake without thinking. I'm becoming healthy, which is to say, imbecile. Another year of this and I'll be pure savage and achieve Nirvana and pleasantly disintegrate in space."

He turned to catch Gibble's stare of revulsion and was surprised into asking, "Why, what's the matter, Gibby?"

"Nothing. I mean—nothing——" said Gibble, removing his stare in a hurry.

"And a mad-headed word-spinnin' bastard you are," said Pat to Carrol. "You'd set a man dithered tryin' to make sense of your talk. What need have you of bein' safe over yonder barrin' bein' run in betimes, or not havin' the price of a drink on you?"

Carrol laughed.

"Well you see, Pat," he said lucidly, "I live in a dark dangerous world where the only safe thing to do is to step on an idea over nothing. I can't get into that safe snug homely place of yours where everything is made of concrete and sheet iron, and you all throw bricks and blows and bullets at each other just for the fun of seeing them bounce harmlessly off again."

"To hell with you. I'd sooner talk to Gibby there for sense, barrin' he has nothin' to talk about."

But Gibble refused to place his stare at the service of either of them. He refused to look at Sadie too. He sat there with little white dents coming out on his face; a compression that left a rejection of concessions potently unuttered.

CHAPTER THIRTEEN.

I'LL be glad when you two loafers are about again," said Carrol. "I hate climbing palm trees and the guavas are running out hereabouts and it's no joke under any terms chasing around in that scrub."

Pat grinned at him. "I'll take over your job with pleasure huntin' fruit with Lady Sadie," said he.

Carrol grimaced discretion behind Gibble's back. "Well, so you can. I'll be glad to get back to a little light carpentering now we have our tool. Consider the joys of real furniture; beds, for example. A square frame lashed with fibre would have the charm of a spring mattress after our doss-heaps."

Gibble glanced up a moment, but repressed a return to optimism.

"Then again, huts," went on the discretionist. "We'll need one for ourselves, as we can't use Sadie's."

"And—er—exactly," said Gibble.

"In fact, as soon as I'm back we'll all start twisting fibre for binding."

"Good," agreed Gibble, perceptibly relieved of brooding.

Sadie came back from where she had been loitering further along the beach and called impatiently, "Come on."

"What about you getting fruit this morning?"

"Absurd! You don't think I'm going to climb palm trees, do you? Come at once."

"Oh, well——"

Carrol resigned himself to exertions for the common good and went off with her, taking with him a brief resurrection of optimism in Gibble.

"And a fine hearty lyin' lad you are, too," said Pat, grinning at Carrol's departing figure.

From darkly brooding, Gibble suddenly uttered the sound of a plucked cork. He got up and began limping about, directing rage at experiments with a sprained ankle.

"Damn the thing," he exclaimed, and hopped in a frenzy.

"A nuisance it is bein' tied by the leg from goin' fruitin'," admitted Pat.

"Damn the bloody thing," vociferated Gibble.

"And that will relieve your feelin's too," said Pat approvingly.

Gibble quivered at him a moment, with chalky dents flickering about a face of beetling scarlet, but compressions failed of utterance. He hopped to the fishing lines and scrambled up some relics of crab for bait and limped dementedly off to the lagoon, letting his ankle have the worst of it.

"And that's bedamned to that," said Pat, having extorted so much diversion from Gibble's antics. He got up and performed aimlessly with his stiff leg, scowling vacantly at a prospect non-existent for the lack of talk.

"Curse Mary Gavan and old Joe Plunket," he said, and stretched himself in the sun to doze.

In a glade of shadows, where the creepers dripped trails of light from above and the grass pricked itself into patterns of green and gold below, Carrol was lecturing Sadie, who sprawled on her back, squandering inattention on him.

"It's all very well saying pooh! Sadie, but those two will be about shortly, and play hell with our honeymoon. As it is, my impersonation of a community worker is wearing dam' thin, and you come and bust it up with a crude demand to come out canoodling just as I had Gibby nicely soothed on the subject of church work. He's been sitting about with the eye of a brooding codfish and I'll swear Pat has been injecting poison into him. Then again, last night! The idea of your lugging me out of bed after midnight!"

"I couldn't sleep. And the moon came up."

"Don't fub it off on the moon. Any more of this sort of thing and your indiscretions will be the talk of the island. People will be saying all sorts of things about us. And don't forget that Pat's a close observer."

"That fool!"

"He's no fool. What he doesn't induce he makes a point of observing from behind a bush."

"Let him."

"Damn it, you can't stop him. And then there's Gibby. I don't like his eye."

"What's it got to do with either of them?"

"Hang it, this isn't Coogee. I'm not looking for competition with those two. Not that I count Gibby in there, but I won't fight Pat if it comes to an argument over precedence."

"Oh, bother Pat."

"No, the point about all this is that we'll have to take more precautions."

He paused, with a grimace. "Precautions! Hell, I wish we *had* taken precautions."

"Oh, shut up, you're always talking."

"And you're never listening. But by ginger, if nothing happens this time I swear. . ."

"Shut up!"

She raised herself to lean over him with a threatening display of even white teeth and extort a hasty protest from him.

"Down! No playing at lions. Stop, that tickles. You are becoming dangerous. Be discreet. Besides, this is too—Hell! don't bite like that. . . ."

Pat and Gibble were about again that week, though Gibble went with a limp and a bandaged ankle. They returned to an active life emanating a certain suspicion that they had taken the community's disasters on themselves for a reward of treachery from the community. Gibble abandoned brooding for a compression of white dents marking resolution, expressed as a claim to Sadie's company. He placed himself about her with a certain ostentation under Carrol's eye. If she loitered forth, he went with her. In defiance of Pat, he took his station on the flat rocks when she went to her beach to swim.

Carrol endorsed these pretensions in private to Sadie.

"Quite right; make a point of seeing a good bit of Gibby. If Pat sees you about with him more than me he'll be put out of action for snooping on us."

"Pooh, I don't mind Gibby," said Sadie, rejecting a need for diplomacy on that or any other score.

Pat also rejected diplomacy for a frank statement of motives in private to Carrol.

"To put the thing fair and square, man to man and face to face it's a liar you are," said he.

"I am not. The situation is the same now as ever it was. Go and hide behind a bush and find out for yourself if you don't believe me."

"It's that cunnin' you are I haven't been able to come

at you, and that's what makes me so sure the wench is connivin' with you."

"Be damned to you. Who gave you the right to supervise this place, anyhow?"

"And be damned to you, Jimmy Carrol, for thinkin' you are goin' to have everything goin' the way it pleases you, makin' hoodlums of me and the queer feller."

Carrol went off a certain distance and sat down.

"You stay where you are," he said. "You're not going to work your temper off on my ribs again. Try it on and, by ginger, the next time I get you in the lagoon I'll drown you."

"To hell with you," roared Pat, exploding.

He stamped up and down a fixed distance from Carrol, hurling impotent punches at him across it.

"That's right, exercise will do you good," said Carrol.

With a familiar gesture of anathema Pat stamped off suddenly into the scrub, punching his way out of sight.

"Damned old lunatic," muttered Carrol. "He needs having trees dropped on him at regular intervals; it seems to soothe him."

He pondered irritably a while and gave that up to stretch comfortably in the shade. These alehouse benches of sun and sand and sea were marvellously sedative. "No doubt I'm getting the trick of islands," thought Carrol, deceived by the lapse of a honeymoon episode. Positive values are apt to be a trifle overdone in these affairs. . . .

From a period of dozing he emerged to discover

Gibble peering at him with a vanishing effect of suspicion.

"Where's Sadie?" he asked.

"Don't know—I thought she was with you."

"I missed her——" Gibble's gaze vacillated about the beach and recalled another absence.

"Where's Pat?"

"Don't know. He was here a while back but he went off in a temper."

"What about?"

"Oh, just one of his schoolgirl vapours. He's in there somewhere."

Gibble's uneasy gaze travelled to the scrub and effected a magnetism on his legs and drew him into it.

"If Pat only decides to put a head on Gibby all will be well," thought Carrol, and dozed off again.

Gibble edged into the scrub, listening and peering and treading with care. Insensibly, his course took a curve that brought him to the other side of Sadie's alcove; the mystery place of her retirements. There, his progress became a crouch; his eye alarmed. Intermittently came a sound of voices out of the scrub. Worming in closer, he heard Pat say:

"If you will not put your foot on me, will you lend me one of your shoes?"

"What for?"

"It's a fancy I have to be holdin' something you feet have trod in."

"You're a fool."

"I am. An' a fool I wish to be, sittin' here lookin' at

you. Will you sit quiet a minute while I kiss your feet."

"Pooh!" was all Sadie said to that.

The pause that followed distracted Gibble. In a frenzy of haste and silence he squirmed in among the bushes till he was able to overlook a section of the rock pool, with Sadie perched on a rock, sedately plaiting her hair. A bush cut off this spectacle at her knees, but by another exercise of squirming he was able to discover Pat stretched at her feet, embracing them.

Possibly Sadie's calmness was the most confounding aspect of this sylvan tableau. She went on doing her hair without haste and without any concern for the prostrate orientalist at her feet. When the plait was finished she tied it with a whisp of fibre and stood up, pushing Pat aside with a foot.

"You're not goin'," he protested.

"Of course, I am. Get up and don't be an idiot."

Pat sat there and stared at her and the expression of his eye was forlorn.

"I don't know how it is you put a twist in me that makes me dithered," said he. "It's not like the way I am with a girl by rights at all."

Sadie did not bother to pooh this triviality away as usual but put her comb carefully in its bark glory box and strolled off, leaving Pat shaking his head mournfully after her.

"It's dithered I am, sure an' all," Gibble heard him announce to the undergrowth.

Gibble wormed his way silently out of hearing, confessing an eye also at the mercy of a confounded mental process.   He found it difficult to think coherently on that peculiar revelation, which angered and appeased the special megalomania of lover in him.   It was portentous and trivial, alarming and reassuring.   Sadie could be approached yet make nothing of approaches, even when those were made on a principle quite outside any conception Gibble had of the way these things are done.   Conventional fiction had defrauded him of the knowledge that he wished to appeal to the beloved for favours on his belly too, and perhaps that accounted for the confusion of mind that applauded and rejected the calm way she had pushed Pat aside with her foot. . . .

He watched them both furtively at the fire that night, hoping to detect an admission of latent depravities.   He put that to himself as hoping that Sadie would express a rejection of depravity in relation to Pat, but Sadie's eyelids were unaware that such an absurd word existed. She took no notice of Pat, but ate her food intent on an inward speculation that contracted her brows at intervals.   Pat only sat trickling sand through his fingers; his signal of a depressed emotion.   When Carrol arrived at leisure for the evening meal and said, "Hello, Irish, got over your temper?" Pat only answered peevishly, "Shut your gob and don't bother me."

But Sadie brought them all back to a standard convention by asking suddenly:

"How long have we been on this island?"

No one had kept count of the days, it seemed, and

all set about trying to calculate them, with a disparity of opinion between a month and two weeks and two months and one week.

"Can't you get closer to it than that?" demanded Sadie.

They could not. Nor could Sadie, with a better clockwork than any of them for computing periods.

CHAPTER FOURTEEN

ON the flat rocks next morning Gibble fished between those uprushes of perturbation and downrushes of depression which mark the incompetent lover premeditating an advance on the beloved.

Reverie had readjusted that episode at the rock pool to imageries of advance not to be rejected, but a great agitation of the spirit kept him from advancing.

He fished till Sadie had swum, sun-baked and retired to the shade to fluff out her hair and prepare it for combing; a ritual that elaborated for her all other deprivations of the toilet. Thereto came Gibble stroll-

184

ing, with a slight inflection of slinking, and seated himself beside her.

"The fish aren't biting," he explained.

Annoying that he had to offer an excuse for joining
her. More annoying that Sadie never saw any significance in his joining her. Finally annoying that having joined her he could find nothing to say to her.

As usual, he watched her from behind the coverts
of irresolute desire, putting himself out of action by
her overwhelming desirability. Light beat up from the
sand and made marvellous tints of her skin, as if light
from within glowed through it. Its essence permeated
her in a radiation of health, as sweetly scented as the
fruits that had replaced a crude dynamic once extracted
from the dead bodies of animals. They had all profited
by a fish and fruit diet in its return of a clarified blood
system.

"My foot's practically all right again," said Gibble
at last, "I shall never forget that night, wondering
what had become of you."

"Pity you didn't think of the cave—plenty of room
there for two."

"I wish I had—it would have been——"

Opportunities like that always clogged his tongue
with unfinished sentences. Sadie hummed, tossing her
hair to left, right and forward, so that her face vanished
and her shoulders were marvellously revealed; a
smooth expanse of girl on which Gibble's eyes fastened
with avidity and alarm. He had but to bend his neck
to kiss it.

"Do you begin to find this island beautiful as Carrol says he does?" he asked hurriedly.

Sadie's face emerged through her hair expressing intolerance.

"Absurd! It's a rotten hole. And that reminds me that nothing has been done about that fire to signal ships. Suppose one were to pass at this very moment, where would we be, running madly about pulling up bushes and the ship out of sight in no time."

"Yes, yes! we really must see about that. I'll start it today."

Sadie's face vanished again, leaving Gibble to the disturbing invitation of her shoulders. There was her hand, too, idly flexible on the sand within a hand's breadth of his. A beautiful hand, broad in the palm, with long smooth fingers and a resolute thumb; five separate embraces at one touch.

"I forgot to ask what you did with that bottle of liquor you got from the boat," said Gibble to the hand.

"I put it in the cave."

"I suppose it's safe there. Still, perhaps it would be better to bury it. You never know; he might go there by chance and find it."

"Who?"

"Pat."

"Why do you want to keep it from him?"

"Oh, he'd drink it at once."

"But we don't want it; I hate spirits."

"Yes, but—he is not to be trusted. I mean, if he was drunk he—you never know what he might do."

Sadie sniffed her usual dismissal of Pat, drunk or otherwise.

"A nuisance, not having an extra comb," she said. "I dare not bring it here for fear of losing it. I did once and nearly went mad hunting for it in the sand. Luckily I got it again, but since that I never bring it out here with me."

She began tying her hair back with a twist of grass, and the movements of her uplifted arms sent little ripples to her nipples, which made two embossed patterns of themselves in her thin singlet, and sent responsive ripples of emotion down Gibble's spine. Now was the moment, with her arms busy and her head turned sideways to him, to lean across and kiss her.

"It won't be long before we have your hut finished and then you'll have a place to keep your things," said Gibble.

"Time enough, too. We want a cupboard or something to keep fruit in. That reminds me that I dreamt about fruit last night. I dreamt that Jimmy and I went up an immense number of stairs to a restaurant on top of a building and all we could get there was fruit to eat and I was in a furious rage because other people were there eating ices and chicken and cutlets and then you were there eating bananas and you came over to me and said, 'I've been saving this banana for you,' and I was so annoyed that I snatched your banana and threw it downstairs."

"Really," said Gibble, and smiled weakly. He wished to quote the popular axiom that dreams go by contraries, but missed that. Still, it was something to have figured in her dreams, even in the posture of having one's banana rejected.

She got up and Gibble reluctantly followed. And he had not kissed her. Such a lost opportunity seemed irremediable in time and space. When alone, this paralysis of resolution confounded him, for when alone he was full of resolution. He worked over its gesture till he was letter perfect in the part of the conquering lover. He would say this, she would say that, which allowed him to say this, whereupon he kissed her. But when with her the cue for a nice introduction of this and that never seemed to arrive, so how could he kiss her?

Yet kiss her he did, and that in a publicity that put any theory of stage cues out of question. They were all cutting grass for thatching in a glade beyond the camp. It was grass that grew in immense tufts like round cushions with elaborate fringes and Sadie sat down on one.

"They wouldn't make bad seats if they were tied round the middle," she said to Gibble, who was cutting grass beside her. He paused to consider the proposal and Sadie, bouncing on her perch, slid off into his arms and he kissed her. He kissed her on the left eyebrow, and it was done before he had time to think of doing it, and he was so startled at having done it that he glanced hastily round at Pat and Carrol to see if they had detected the tremendous act. But they were busy with their job and a marvel passed unnoticed. Sadie failed

were so mysterious, so removed. How was I to approach you? Yet I had a premonition: that is the one
and only woman on earth. And now I touch you,—I
hold you,—you who are like some wondrous being
from another sphere——"

"Well, I will say I never could stand being like
everybody else, and that was a constant difference of
opinion between my sister Fanny and me, because Fanny
always rushed the last thing out simply because everyone else was doing it, making an awful mess of our
front lawn with miniature golf and if ever there was an
imbecile game *that* is, and not content with bobbing she
must go and get Eton-cropped, the turnip-topped little
idiot—even *she* could see it didn't suit her, as I told
her from the first."

"How wise you are. It would have been sacrilege to
cut a single lock of this wonderful hair."

Very right and proper all this, as Sadie's eyelids endorsed. They found nothing exotic in these transcripts
of her desirability. Without troubling an authority in
third-rate fiction, she was aware of its idiom, which
Carrol's inadequate literary taste had failed to supply.
Sadie was a rational girl, and rejected any assumption
that being mugged about and raved about implied either
a concession or a responsibility on her part. That is to
say, she did not think about the business at all. It was
a pleasing accompaniment to hair tossing to be embraced over areas that excluded contentious politics
about the possession of breasts and legs. Adoration for
the wonder and mystery of her being was the duty of

all men, and Gibble was all men, or at least a few millions of them.

"Tell me, tell me,—though I hardly dare ask it—tell me that you care a little for me."

"Of course, I do, Gibby."

If Sadie had said, "Of course, I don't," her intonation would have been the same.

"My wonderful girl," said Gibble fervently. . . .

Pat strolled out on the other beach where Carrol was working and grinned at him with great satisfaction.

"Things is not goin' so much your way as you think, Jimmy Carrol," said he.

"Indeed?"

"No, indeed.   I've this minute come from watchin' Gibby buzzin' away at her on the beach yonder and it's workin' up his leather he'll be between this and a pig's whisper if you ask my opinion."

"I don't," said Carrol, grinning.   "My own opinion is that Gibby isn't up to Sadie's standard as a sparring partner; he wouldn't last one round."

He went on chipping and finished that piece of wood and picked up another, watched with suspicion by Pat.

"It's such a trained liar you are a man might think you didn't care a turnip who had the wench," said he.

"Of course, I do; haven't I been putting up a wrestling match with her on my own account?"

"You've wrestled yourself into a look of bein' mighty pleased at bein' beaten by her.   And the wench has a satisfied look in her eye for the same reason."

He went off a pace or two and turned to regard Carrol with pardonable annoyance.

"You'll understand that I'm not taken by your talk at all," he said.

"That's understood," Carrol assured him.

He went on chipping till Pat had gone off into the scrub again, which allowed him to drop the axe for an interval of meditation and an expression of annoyance, disposed of by a sudden return to chipping.

"No, I'm damned if I will," he muttered. "If she likes to act the goat with that goat, let her. I will not let that sort of rot disturb my island opium den."

But it did, all the same. In ten minutes' time he had abandoned chipping and had vacillated to the headland with an irritated suspicion of being under inspection by Pat. As an accident of strolling he got round the headland and discovered Sadie and Gibble seated in the shade and loitered across to join them.

Sadie's presence there was understood and Gibble accounted for the blush that lingered in faltering gradations to his ribs by explaining that the fish were not biting.

"Not biting, aren't they?" said Carrol, and almost added, "Perhaps Sadie is," but repressed the indiscretion. An effect of hostility, nevertheless, sent another flush to Gibble's ears.

"No, they're not biting," he said abruptly.

"Well, well," said Carrol.

He lay down, stretched himself, and there remained, imposing on Gibble a conviction of malicious intrusion.

It accomplished at once the rebellions of jealousy. Gibble's humility as lover stopped short only at the beloved; elsewhere it arrived at a monstrous arrogance that could not tolerate any approach to her by others. It gave him a thrill of agony to note that Carrol's arm touched Sadie's thigh. He wished to snatch her quiveringly from an impure contact, which she seemed strangely unaware of. A momentous silence endured because Carrol pretended to doze and Gibble continued to abhor him. He tried to extract from Sadie's eyes an admission that this was a vile intrusion on their perfect love, but Sadie appeared to be unaware of that too. When she rose to walk back to the camp, he stepped in between her and Carrol. At the midday meal he fussed about her, serving her with food. When she retired after it to her alcove he hung about the edge of the scrub till she returned, and hastened at once to join her. He assisted at thatching the hut because she sat to watch them at work, but the moment she strolled off he dropped what he was doing to run after her. It was an obvious torture to be separated from her even by a space of sand. And he went through those antics flagrantly unaware that they exposed the nature of his obsession.

"Will you only look at him?" said Pat, enchanted. "He'll be cockin' his leg at the next stump he's that randy."

"The blithering ass—it's gone to his head," said Carrol.

He was enraged at Gibble's infatuation and enraged

at finding himself so disturbed by it, and both conflictions were dammed up because Pat was grinning there as their audience.

"Well, well, well!" said Pat. "It's beknowns there's a streak of billygoat in them parsons, the which has got them so set agen a bit of the same enjoyment in other people. We'll have the laugh of the world over this in my opinion and I'll not miss any fun is goin'."

With a wink he went off into the scrub and Carrol in a rage went back to thatching. Under no persuasion would he exhibit himself as third buffoon for Pat's diversion, and endured with seething discretion the return of Gibble and Sadie. Perhaps the most exasperating part of the business was Sadie's superb unawareness that Gibble was going on about her like a uxorious poodle. . . .

He waited till Gibble was wood gathering next morning to go round through the scrub to Sadie's alcove and draw her away into the bush to have a row with her in private.

". . . Discretion is all very well but, dam' it, this sort of thing is a bit over the odds. I told you to be seen about with that runt but I never told you to get mugged about by him and I won't stand it."

"Oh, indeed!"

"I won't, that's flat."

"Well, don't."

"Look here, you put a stop to this foolery before it goes any further."

"A nice fuss over nothing.   There's not the slightest harm in Gibby."

"Harm! the idiot's gone ratty over you."

Sadie preened herself with calm detachment from the laws of nature on that score.

"I suppose *I'm* responsible for that."

"You are; you've encouraged the imbecile."

"Drivel."

"All right, you can go to hell."

He kissed her with hatred under the chin; Sadie nipped his ear; these uproars go on a prescribed ritual. Five minutes later Carrol said hurriedly, "I don't trust this part—let's get away into a safe place. . . ."

Gibble put the fire in order and hurried down to Sadie's beach, but it was empty.   He ran back to her alcove but that was empty too.   Neither Pat nor Carrol was to be seen either.   He sped along the edge of the scrub calling "Sadie" at intervals in a voice of tender modulation.   To his annoyance it produced, not Sadie, but Pat, who came suddenly out of the bushes and beckoned Gibble to him.

"Come here a bit and I'll tell you where she is," he called.

Gibble frowned at an obnoxious partisan but moved towards him.   Pat lugged him into the scrub, leading the way with a fulsome show of zeal in Gibble's service.

"She's in that bit of a dip yonder beyont them banyans," said he.   "Tread soft, now, and give her a surprise."

With a wink of encouragement he dodged away, and
Gibble went forward, treading not so softly that Carrol
had time to slide off into the scrub, muttering impre-
cations. When Gibble emerged she was sitting up, staring her widest. . . .

"My wonderful girl," said Gibble, darting to embrace her.

"Absurd," exclaimed Sadie, and pushed him off.
A million popular novels crashed on Gibble's skull
and stunned him.

"But, but, but,—what—why—" he stammered.

Sadie tugged her petticoat viciously down, gripped
her knees and refused to look at him. Her posture was
rigid with offended propriety, and Gibble sat back on
his hams and gaped at her.

"But—but—Sadie, what have I done?"

"Nothing!"

"Then why——"

"I object to being followed about, that's all."

Gibble got up and backed slowly to the scrub. His gaze was vacant, save for a lurking ingredient of terror. It stultified other alarms at her pose of repudiation and her staring eyes that refused to look at him. Yet it exerted a fascination that also refused to let him leave her. He faltered there helplessly, staring from her to the packed foliage, at which he automatically listened. . . .

But he had to get it out and did so.

"Sadie, tell me the truth. Are you and Carrol—is Carrol—are you—are you and Carrol—you know what I mean."

"What do you mean?"

"I mean—I must know. What have you given to him?"

Sadie only twitched an impatient shoulder. An up-rush of emotion forced Gibble to raise his voice.

"I must know," he shouted. "I won't be deceived. You let me kiss you—you must love me. You said you did. After this—anyone else—impossible—I would kill him."

He gesticulated wildly at the scrub, darted at Sadie and grappled with her.

"You are mine—I must have you—I will——"

He had her, to the extent of a brief tussle, which thrust him off ruthlessly.

"Absurd!" was all Sadie said, rigidly adjusting her petticoat.

Gibble threw himself down and wept discordantly, clutching at the ground with demented fingers. In itself, it was a peculiar exhibition, warranting attention even outside the necessary abasements of a lover, but Sadie did not give it a glance.

"I simply will not be dictated to by anybody on this island," she said, not at Gibble, but as announcing a general principle.

But Gibble was incapable of obeying any principle save those disruptions which had exploded a perfect love affair. He did not refuse to leave Sadie; he was incapable of doing so. He had to be tortured by her if there was no other way of achieving contact with her. He lay there and grovelled and Sadie, in a rage, got up and left him. Instantly Gibble scrambled up and followed her, insensible of his beslobbered eyes.

Sadie came out on her beach and without counting Gibble present dropped off her clothes and plunged into the water, swimming out to the reef, where she remained; a sanctuary from fools. Gibble stared fixedly at her for a long time and at last drifted to the headland, where he sat down. Within a brief interval Carrol came out of the scrub, scowled at Gibble, and walked to the other end of the beach and seated himself, as a pendent lover in waiting. Upon that Pat appeared, obnoxiously innocent of a situation he had ingeniously dramatized. He patrolled the beach elegantly, as a gentleman taking his leisure to enjoy the air.

At that grouping all remained. When Sadie emerged from the water, rudely unaware of them, snatched on her clothes and returned to the camp, she was escorted by a procession of three, walking at stated distances from each other.

Gibble was responsible for keeping the group at that tension. From brooding over all the offences of jealousy, he had arrived at a fixed justification of his mighty wrongs, which he made no attempt to disguise. Its defiance was stated; where Sadie went, he went. He did not join her, but followed at a short distance, and so remained, a sheep-like obstinacy that was impervious to Sadie's starings, Carrol's scowls and Pat's grins. He also threw over all further responsibility to a treacherous community. Carrol had to keep the fire going and spend the afternoon fishing, which at least got him away from attending to Gibble's dementia. Sadie cleared off to her alcove, which forced Gibble to keep lurking about the scrub, lest treachery proposed another secret assignation there. Pat refused to leave the camp, so that he could inspect the home-made diversion of Gibble's antics at his ease. His pose of hearty good-fellowship over the business was as annoying to Carrol as Gibble's emanation at them as convicted malignants.

Still, he allowed himself to eat with them. There was that about his partaking of food which made more awful still his rejection of any social concession to a social function. Sadie rejected it too, but that was be-

cause her thoughts were busy over other things, which
contracted her brows, and forced her shoulders up into
an impatient shiver.   It appeared to be as an after-
thought that she discovered herself half-way through
a fish and cast it from her with a lack of interest.   Half
a plantain followed it.   She got up and drifted to the
lagoon and remained staring for a long time at the dying reflection of the sky.   When she turned to discover
the martyr to baseness still on guard behind her she uttered a hissing rejection of him and swished off to her
couch.

Gibble stood about.   By degrees he edged into the
firelight and stood about there.   Since Sadie had gone
that justification of wrongs had to be seen by someone
and Pat, for one, gave it a hearty welcome.

"Come along, Gibby lad, and sit you down and ease
your feelin's, for here is Jimmy like a man and a
brother waitin' to have it out with you face to face and
heart to heart."

"Shut up," hissed Carrol.   "Your bloody sense of
humour is as bad as a demented lack of it at present
blighting our happy island home."

"Well, for God's sake, isn't there some things needs
grinnin' at in this place?"

"Yes; they're so dam' funny you can't laugh at
them."

"I can, begob."

"I can't; asylums are only funny when you don't
have to live in them."

From brooding, Gibble's eye suddenly flared.   He

came to the fire, gesticulating at Carrol. As usual, combustion sent his voice up to a shout.

"You! you—who are you to take a superior air to me?"

"To you? You've got swelled head; I never put you up as a standard of intelligence."

"Pah! All this talk! Don't think I've been taken in by it. If you only knew what I've been thinking about you. I've watched you; I've seen through you. All this pose of superiority and nothing to show for it."

That punctured Carrol vitally, touching as it did the sensitive core of a frustrate.

"No, nothing," he snarled. "That's something for you to crow over, you blasted convict system complex. A fat chance anyone in Australia has had of doing anything worth doing with a few million of your sort ready to howl like dingos to have it suppressed."

"Arrogance and incompetence," shouted Gibble. "That's what you are—a typical waster of an Australian."

"Inferiority and suppressed lust; that's what you are, you damned wowser," yelled Carrol.

"Into him, Jimmy boy; pass him another, Gibby lad," shouted Pat in high glee.

"To hell with you," raged Carrol at him. "If you had to get knocked overboard by a damned wowser, why the hell didn't you do the decent thing and drown him and yourself too?"

"Your temper's up and now you're talkin'," approved

Pat. "What the pair of you needs is a fair go face to face will ease your hearts an' feelin's."

"Oh, to blazes," shouted Carrol.

But Gibble's pink scowl and an awful compression of white dents was an irresistible affront and he leaped up, making round the fire to get at it. Gibble put himself in a cataleptic posture awaiting combat. . . .

Sadie was suddenly in the firelight, her eyes dilated with anger.

"What do you mean by making this filthy uproar?" she exclaimed. "Impossible to get a wink of sleep with it. Stop it this instant."

Her temper was at a higher tension than Carrol's or Gibble's and quelled them both. They stood there lowering, fatuously arrested at a fine male crescendo.

"Go to bed, instantly," stamped Sadie at them.

They went, such are the subjective compulsions generated in the male. Sadie watched them both under cover of their shelters and turned on Pat.

"You too," she said.

Pat made a resigned gesture, as one most unjustly robbed of a well-earned diversion, but he went off to his lair, leaving Sadie alone with the fire, which showed her angry eyes still unappeased by surrender to them. . . .

As an altogether overdone anticlimax it rained heavily before dawn and drove them all for shelter to the unfinished hut, which leaked abominably, and kept them in active discomfort till a grey light filtered through a grey sky came over the sea rim and showed them sitting in the drips. They all looked glum enough, but Gibble's expression was fixed in dents that excluded any possible return to the amenities.

CHAPTER FIFTEEN

I T RAINED the most part of next day and kept
them busy patching at the hut, and gathering into
it enough dried stuff to sleep on, and by nightfall
they were securely enough under shelter, save for a
drip or two. A fire was built at the open end under
a lean-to of boughs, and a pile of wood was carried
in to keep it going through the night.

These matters kept them too busy to concentrate on disruptions of the spirit, which must be understood to exclude Gibble, who concentrated on nothing else. He worked silently at the thatching, since even a blighted life may object to sitting in rain drips, but he did nothing else. His stare now rejected any knowledge of Carrol's existence. Sadie and Pat were admitted to have being within a certain radius of their own feet, but Carrol was wiped from the earth's surface. The only concession he made to group movement was to maintain the now fixed rule of his just resentments: where Sadie went, he walked a regulation space behind her.

Pat was induced to pull down a few coconuts and Carrol took a wet hour off on the reef fishing. He had left his sodden trousers before the fire to dry, and came back naked and dripping to stand before it and dry his skin, which almost caused Gibble's opaque stare to account for an unseen offence somewhere.

Sadie was given one side of the hut and the other three stretched themselves in a row opposite her. When Carrol woke in the night to put more wood on the fire, Gibble's head, on a stalk of neck, rose up to watch an unacknowledged presence. He was guarding his ruined episode of love from approaches even there, it seemed.

The sun shone next day and restored them to the open again, if not to freedom of movement there. Gibble refused to ratify that. It was clear that a conviction of monstrous injustice done him had detached him from any sense of a rational grouping in their isolation. It also destroyed the group's ability to rationalize itself. Ease of address was impossible under the smouldering resentment of his eye. He came to meals and demolished their one stable social function. He renounced all claims of service to a community ostracized beyond the redemption of his mighty wrongs. He did nothing but stand about within a radius of Sadie and brood in ostentatious isolation.

To all that Sadie paid only a minor attention; like Gibble, she seemed to have a private quantity of wrongs to brood on, which left her irritated and distrait, and rejecting talk. She spent a lot of time in her alcove, with Gibble on guard. But even he was forced to make a brief sanitary excursion into the scrub at intervals and Carrol snatched one to say, "Come on, Sadie, scoot off now while the lunatic is off duty."

"Oh, don't bother me," said Sadie impatiently.

"But hang it, Sadie, what *is* the matter?"

"Nothing."

She snapped that at him and walked away, and Carrol ran after her in alarm.

"You must tell me; what is it?"

"I tell you I simply don't want to be bothered with any of you."

Gibble burst out of the scrub then and took his stand, detecting a conspiracy in the very making, and Carrol went off spitting expletives. The domesticity of the camp now fell on him, for Pat abandoned himself to a conception of anarchy and refused to do anything except climb for coconuts; an exercise which he enjoyed as an ostentation of muscular power. He hung about the camp, always ready with a blandishment to soothe Sadie's temper. . . .

They had three days of that and everybody's nerves began to go. Carrol was most perturbed of all; he now had a horrid suspicion of what was causing Sadie's secret irritation and wished, and was terrified, to have it confirmed. But he got no chance to, night or day. Even if he moved on his brushwood couch a corresponding crackle of twigs came from Gibble's lair. The wretch seemed to do without sleep. Proposals to detach Sadie for that midnight were quite defeated. Nor could he sneak an interview during her bathing hour. Gibble brooded there with special pertinacity. Sadie might emerge to slap the water from her splendid figure in a fury, and sun-bake with a vicious rejection of being overlooked—the sentinel of gloom remained at his post. . . .

For even Sadie's preoccupation over a latent alarm gave way before this incessant haunting. Her alcove was no longer a privacy, and any movement into the scrub might detect Gibble brooding at her behind a bush. If she waved him off he merely stood off, and that was all. Her other face was now the only one she wore, and her tattered chemise could hardly support the expansions of her temper. Moreover, the wretch put her to a great deal of discomfort over a secret ritual that the crude economics of the boat had been forced to dispense with, and even Montaigne's

almost perfect equanimity confessed that it could not
endure intrusion at such a moment. . . .

She came to the midday meal on that third day barely
controlling explosive outcries. Her lips were clamped
and her eyes distended, and she only snatched a plantain to take one bite that choked her power to eat
another mouthful. With that she hurled the fruit from
her and sprang up, exclaiming:

"God! Jimmy Carrol, I hate you."

Before Pat or Carrol could collate the rational of

that accusation she turned and dashed back into the scrub, leaving them gaping. Further along the beach Gibble stood arrested too, bemused for the moment from brooding.

There Carrol's nerves threw up their job and he hurled down his untouched food too.

"God in hell, but this is beyond bearing. That imbecile's got us at his mercy; he's destroyed whatever illusion of privacy we had. There's no living under such a restraint, and what the hell can we do with him?"

"Give him a punch in the slats, of course."

"Go and punch him yourself; it's your speciality."

"What call have I to be interferin' between the pair of yous, havin' no rights on Lady Sadie at all. The pair of yous is to fight it out, and that's the opinion I give you. I'm not sayin' who I'd back to win but that's neither here nor there. The queer feller has a temper and that's in his favour, but if you rattle him up a bit with a thump or two in the nose I doubt he'd take much beatin'. But a beatin' he needs, sure and all. Never have it said of you, Jimmy boy, you let your ill feelin's interfere with givin' a ditherin' runt like that his proper needs."

"Oh, go to blazes," said Carrol sourly, and got up to walk off across the beach.

Pat watched him go with derision, and turned to see Gibble hasting into the scrub. With Carrol gone one way and Sadie another treachery might even now be defeating the justification of his wrongs. Pat strolled into the scrub a pace or two, watching Gibble craning here and there. Then he stopped abruptly and Sadie appeared. . . .

Perhaps just such a hair trigger as Gibble's intrusion was needed at that moment, for she came at him flaming with fury.

"You dare come prying, sneaking here again, you wretched creature," she screamed. "You dare—you dare——"

Gibble backed away, mesmerized by the fury of her eye. He backed into a thorn bush, shot from that into a confession of defeat and bolted, with Sadie storming behind him, "Get out, you dare come sneaking after me again . . ."

Pat picked up Gibble in transit and wheeled him about, roughing him by the arm.

"Come on now out of this before she comes at you and kills you, which is what you deserve for stickin' your nose into her private affairs. If she doesn't do it I'll do it for her, so mind that while you have a head on you. Run after Jimmy yonder, you that must be tailin' somebody. He's made it up belike to meet her there, and that'll keep you busy nosin' after him."

He gave Gibble a heave that sent him staggering down the sand to fall, pick himself up again, and hurry on, without looking back. Sadie had arrived to watch the ejectment, like a goddess from Valhalla seeing doom meted to an impious wretch. She was so angry that she breathed in gasps, and Pat put a soothing arm round her.

"That's over and done with and you'll not be troubled by Gibby the Goat again, for if he does I give you me word I'll put him in the lagoon and leave him there."

Sadie got her breath back with a long quivering sigh that carried her anger away too and left her suddenly weak. She flopped down on the sand with her head on her knees and burst into tears. Pat kneeled by her, cajoling and petting her.

"Let it go, then, Sadie darlin', and ease your heart and that's your need, and I'm another, to keep them hoodlums from botherin' the life out of you. Never a lie in it, there's only one man here, and it's him would give the breath of his life to kiss your feet. . . ."

Gibble reached the headland without looking back. His mind was in great confusion, and the only salient impression it retained was a threat of violence in Pat's powerful grasp. It displaced a concept of wrongs done for a wrong that might be done, and remained at that till he came round the headland to the other beach and caught sight of Carrol's figure disappearing into the scrub at its far end. Instantly his mind clicked back to its obsession at the spectacle of a hated rival and treachery was alive again. He hurried for fear of losing Carrol in the bush.

But Carrol had continued on across the space of thick growth to that barren promontory and his bolt-hole, into which he crawled to repeat his creed of isolation in desperate terms.

". . . I will—by God I will—I'll clear out to the

other side of the island. This sort of thing is plain
bedlam; there's no living without some agreement on
a theory of living and that blighted Gibble . . .

"And Sadie! Hell! hell—hell—hell! If she's caught
we're all damned. Idiot that I was; drivelling imbecile, to take a risk like that, with a moral certainty that
it *must* go wrong. Only self-hypnotism can account
for such blind folly. Curse that storm! But for that,
I'll swear I would have been careful. . . .

"And those other two—when they know. Two complete irresponsibles. I don't know which is the worst.
I could settle Gibble, but as for Pat . . ."

He gave that up to add explosively, "Hell, I won't
think of this; I'll go dotty."

A protective attack of mental inertia arrived here
to blank out an impossible future, and he lay on his
back and let the blue dome of the sky hypnotize the
exertion of thinking. From that he was presently detached by his ears, which suggested that stealthy sounds
were going about somewhere.

Gibble had glimpsed Carrol disappear in that direction, and he was treading with Indian caution and peering everywhere for him, so that Carrol's head coming
suddenly out of the earth confounded him.

"Oh, you, is it?" said Carrol politely. "Did they
leave the gate open or did you climb over the wall?"

At that, Gibble's frown compressed its dents and so
remained. Carrol got out of his burrow and eyed him
with distaste. From that, he concluded to temporize

a little with discretion again and resumed its intonation of frankness.

"Look here, Gibble, just put aside personal rancour a moment and realize what you are doing. You are knocking whatever security we have here into a cocked hat. It won't work. You are setting up claims to a privilege that can't be maintained; that is, unless you are able to enforce them by strength."

Gibble lowered at that a moment to scent out its special offence.

"What do you mean by that? A threat——"

"Rot! Can't you see that by busting up life socially you've also destroyed its economic stability."

"And who has done that? You! You!"

"Rubbish!"

"You have, you've tried to get Sadie away from me and keep her yourself. You have."

"Well, put it that way if you like, but I haven't tried to impose any mad-headed restrictions on you doing the same thing if you can."

"You have. You've turned her against me. She was all right to me and then suddenly—You must have done something—said something——"

"Rot! Whatever was done was done by you. You made a pest of yourself at—But look here, that's not the point. I'm not denying your right to Sadie, if you can establish it. Or anyone else's right, for that matter. But that's a private affair between you and her; you can't make a public announcement of wrongs about it. Go and have it out with Sadie, but get this resentment bug out of your mind and do your fair share of work and keep up a decent show of good humour. You've simply *got* to do it, or the whole show will go to pot."

Gibble pondered, turning suspicion from Carrol to the sea rim and back to Carrol. But the mulish obstinacy of his frown remained and confirmed the inductions of treachery, and as usual, sent his voice up to a shout.

"What does all this mean! Talk—make me your dupe—smooth over everything so that you can get her away from me——"

"Oh, go to hell."

Carrol turned and walked off, leaving Gibble in a pose of arrested gesticulation. He dropped his arm, stared a moment, and fell into step behind Carrol, walking some twenty paces in the rear. Carrol scowled at the sound of this fanatic trailing, which demolished the theory of a rational earth.

They arrived thus round the headland and across the beach to the camp, where Pat and Sadie made a group of two that disregarded the arrival of two others. Sadie sat with her chin on her fists, staring at the sea, and Pat stood a space behind her, marking her with the frustrated air of one who has talked but not been listened to. He scratched his head and rasped his chin and seemed to give it up.

Carrol and Gibble arrived and stood and looked, and Pat looked at them and Sadie looked at nobody. She frowned intently at whatever speculation it was that evaded analysis, and her disregard for the others was so patent that it suspended their ability to command attention.

Pat was the first to throw over responsibility for the rejections of a sensible man, and dropped on the sand with a peevish gesture.

"A mad-headed lot the lot of you are an' that includes everybody," he said, with a forensic particularity directed at Sadie, who took no notice of it.

Carrol stared at both of them without being able to decide what sort of disunion of opinion or personality lay between them. He felt suddenly too used up to bother about it, as if all the stores of emotion had been extracted from his joints as well as his mind, and lay down with a feeble sigh of "Oh, hell."

Gibble stood, left out of an anticlimax that no longer counted him a factor. He frowned vacantly from one to the other, waiting for someone to justify his mislaid martyrdom.

No one did. Sadie dropped her hands to turn and discover three fools but not to identify them. She stood up and looked round her. The fire was out, no one had fished that day, and there were two coconuts in stock. These she picked up and went off into the scrub to her alcove, leaving a flat collapse of the male ego behind her.

CHAPTER SIXTEEN

BUT they had to eat, and that restored a certain convention to their day. It was a depressed one. Pat was sullen and drifted abortively about, going from one end of the beach to the other, and making that gesture of anathema at sea and sky. At last he went into the scrub and stayed there, for he was seen no more that day.

Carrol relit the fire and gathered wood and went for fruit, leaving Gibble to the empty beach. Sadie was out of sight too, but proposals to investigate that quite failed Gibble.   A collective emotion had lapsed and stranded him without initiative, and he looked vacantly about the beach as if trying to find out what had become of a monstrous injustice.   From that he went furtively to the fishing lines and searched out a crab for bait and moved off to the reef where he squatted and fished and tried to find out where the potency of his awful wrongs had got to. . . .

The three of them gathered for the evening meal in silence.   Carrol maintained it by ignoring Gibble and not speaking to Sadie, but behind Gibble's back he signalled at the scrub to her, implying that they must meet there later.   Sadie accepted that by an indifferent nod that dismissed any significance in meeting him there or elsewhere. . . .

When he drifted off across the beach in the dusk Gibble discovered an awful ill-ease alone with Sadie. The idiom of a perfect love affair had vanished with its monstrous wrongs and he could think of nothing to say to her.   What he wanted to do was throw himself at her feet and wallow in abasement for a gift of tenderness, but Sadie's indifferent mask seemed to forget he was there.   He looked furtively at her, aghast at the awful distance between them.   He was alone with her and the opportunity perfect to crave forgiveness and its stress of emotion pressed on him the illusion that if he did not speak now the chance was gone forever.   But Sadie stood up before he could speak and he stared helplessly after her as she loitered to the scrub and vanished. . . .

A radiance stole up from the sea rim where the moon was rising but it was dark in the woods and Carrol stumbled and floundered his way round to Sadie's pool, where she was seated on a rock, a dim shape in the filtered darkness. Carrol took her arm to lead her into the bush, whispering, "Let us get away where we can talk this out, Sadie. . . ."

Talk!

In a little open glade often used by them the moon came up to find Carrol talking, and he talked in the hurried emphatic tones of one who seeks to persuade himself out of an uneasy conscience.

". . . I've worked it out all ways, Sadie, and the best I can think of is to tell those two the plain truth and make them understand that they've bloody well got to behave rationally about it. I think it would work, or at least—Anyway, if it doesn't we'll have to square one and put the other out of action that way, if it comes to a row. That means squaring Gibble, of course, as Pat's unmanageable when he does his block in. We'll have to bank on Gibby by working him up as a noble-minded parson. He ought to come at the pose of protecting helpless womanhood, if he can be induced to keep his private asylum under. Anyway, you'd better leave it to me to put it to those two. . . ."

Sadie suddenly disposed of these wise maunderings by saying scornfully:

"You. What's it got to do with you?"

"Eh! what?"

"You don't have to have the kid."

"But hang it, I want to do what I can to help the infernal business."

"And what *can* you do?"

"Well, I can do something to fix those other two."

Sadie sniffed. Then she said emphatically:

"I won't be bothered by such rot. You kindly mind your own business, Jimmy Carrol, and don't you dare say a word to those other two about this."

"But hang it, Sadie . . ."

The moon rose at its full and now the night was lovely, relieved of isolation in space. A gracious message from that magnificent globe suspended over the sea of security from the unknown.

The beach at least picked it up, ghosted in silver, but the dark woods rejected it, silent and inscrutable. Gibble rejected it too, seated on the sand with his hands gripping his ankles and his chin on his knees and his eyes fixed on the moon's glittering message across the sea.

Behind him the camp fire blurred a patch of warmth in the moon's cool blueness. There was no one there. No one to the right of the beach, no one to the left. Gibble only, seated midway between its curving horns of sand.

He leaped up suddenly and began to move rapidly along the edge of the scrub, stopping at intervals to listen and hasten on again. Round the headland to the other beach, hurrying and stopping, listening and hurrying . . . Only the sly communion of leaves came back to him, whispering of secrets hidden in their shadows.

He sped back to the camp again, pausing only when the leaves deceived him into snatching at their message. They were amused at this distracted eavesdropper, and made up horrid little fantasies for his ears: sighs, kisses, and the breathless ribaldries of two lovers.

He threw himself down, rolling over and over and beating at the sand with fists and feet. The leaves ceased their whispering and looked on astonished at this exhibition. When he sat up again, all was silent, and once more he gripped his ankles, dug his chin between his knees, and stared at the moon's silver path of lies across the sea.

In short, treachery was alive again, and Gibble's dream of abasement and its rewards at Sadie's feet had gone to pieces in the monstrous wrongs of a deceived lover. He had been alone with them on that empty beach for an hour, and they worked their ruthless antic of impotent revenges on him.

Once more his head shot up, listening. Voices! They were coming back. Then he frowned, identifying not voices, but a voice, and that singing. It chanted from somewhere up the headland and down to the palm shadows of the beach, and the words it sang came clearly on the still air:

"March past the Forty-second,
  March past the Forty-four,
  March past the bare-a ... d b ..... s

Comin' from Ashantee War.
Some of them had Highlan' bonnets,
Some of them had none at aw,
Some had kilts and others hadn't,
Them was Highlan' Johnnies raw.
March past———"

It was Pat who thus diverted the night with song,
announcing that it beheld contentments of the spirit.
He came into the moonlight walking expansively, and
with the tread of conquest. At the sight of Gibble
seated there humped up on the sand his good humour
was vastly exhilarated.

"It's Gibby the Goat," he roared. "It's the lad
with the tramp's whiskers for all the world like a belly-
achin' Jasus. Come on now and let me have some
fun out of you to prove it's not a gutful of grunts
you are."

He laid playful hands on Gibble, assisting him to
rise that they might lightly dance together. This proposal was a little misinterpreted by Gibble, who con-
ceived himself plucked aloft by the neck to be tossed
about by awful forces and whizzed back to earth again
with stunning effect.

"Stop—stop—" he gasped, crawfishing madly from
advances plainly bent on murder.

"Will you dance with me or will you not?" demanded Pat. "Ye won't! Of course, you won't.
You've no more fun in you than a crablouse. It's a

dose of jollop you want, to give you something to squitter about."

He forgot that to throw himself down with an almighty thump and laugh enormously. He laughed as at a jest, patent in humour, but hidden from less subtle perceptions than his own. By that time Gibble had recovered his breath and was able to diagnose an aroma which he had been too busy to investigate.

"You're drunk—you found that liquor," he exclaimed.

"You've hit it. And I have to thank you puttin' it by so nice for me. The last place I thought of lookin' for it, an' me diggin' round every palm tree on the beach, thinkin' you had it buried on me."

He laughed again and threw up his legs and arms to wallop them back on the sand.

"Would you ever think a man's mind would play him such a trick? I clean forgot boat's regulations for supplies in case of sudden disaster at sea. A good joke you put on me, keepin' that bottle so dark. It never crossed me mind till I seen you in a lather over them two divin' for it from the boat. But I have the laugh on you this minute. A nice peaceful booze-up I've had, just tricklin' it down and wonderin' I never come to find the taste of it so good before. But it's not gettin' the fun out of it we should be. I've a mind we might wrestle a bit, if I give you a hand in."

"No-no, certainly not," exclaimed Gibble, crawfishing in alarm.

"Ye won't. Did ever a man have to put up with

such a grevious runt, with your tramp's whiskers and all? You'll sing a bit with me, then."

He reached over and pulled Gibble carelessly to him by by the foot, upending him again as if he were a mechanical figure requiring external adjustment.

"The words is these, and you'll bear in mind it's a quick march and take your time accordin'. It's me that starts it, and you that comes in at the March Past."

He lined out the chant, making Gibble repeat the words distractedly after him, and that done, burst loudly into song.

"You're not singin' at all," he said, admonishing Gibble with a petulance that plunged him nose down in the sand. In a frenzy of self-preservation Gibble galloped on all fours to the edge of the scrub and rose panting, ready to flee at further approaches from the gay one.

"Come back," commanded Pat. "Ye won't, of course, you won't. You've neither feelin's nor kindness in you. I've a mind to hold you face down in the lagoon."

He stood there glaring about the empty beach, disgracefully blank of festive resources.

"Where's Jimmy? And Lady Sadie? I have it—he's got her away with him. And why shouldn't he? I'll give him that much in. A smart feller he is. And a lyin' cunnin' bastard he is too. I have that agen him. Why should not the pair of us have her, or all three in justice and reason? He's not for sharin'

her at all.   His idea is to have the pickin's and us
to have the leavin's and dam' little leavin's at that.
I'll not have it.   I'll not be flumdoodled a minute
longer, by him or her either.   She's one will pick you
up and drop you in her whims and fancies too.   I'll
not put up with it.   If he will not hear reason, I'll
knock the face off him."

He strode off into the scrub, seeming to know where
to find those two.   Gibble darted after him, but
stopped, listening to the sounds of his passage through
the bush.   From that he was thrown into a flurry of
indecision, darting back to the camp and hurrying here
and there for something he failed to find.   He snatched
up a stick, but threw that down for a lump of coral. . . .

It was hard to distinguish a sudden hubbub of voices
in the scrub from the hubbub in his mind and the
thudding of his heart, but he ran towards it, bending
and dodging and keeping under cover.   In that little
glade the moonlight was brilliant and he went down
behind a bush, craning a distracted neck.

Pat had Sadie gripped to him by one arm, over
which she bent and struggled.   His feet were strongly
planted and he lunged at Carrol with his other arm,
keeping him skipping back at each advance.   All were
shouting.

"Stop it!—Drop it!—Will you let go, you beast?—
Have sense, you idiot.—Let me at you a minute to
paste the head off you, ye bastard——"

Pat left Carrol a moment to toss Sadie off her feet

and take a fresh grip of her, making nothing of the punches she hammered at him.

"I'll give you me last word," he said. "The pair of us is goin' off from here this minute. If you come after us I'll kill you. Will you not hear reason or will you be off before I do it?"

"I won't, of course, I won't. Don't be an ass and let Sadie go at once. You can't do anything with the two of us against you. If you try it on I'll stun you from behind."

"Then I'll kill you now," roared Pat, and made exertions truly heroic dragging Sadie about the clearing to get at Carrol, who dodged all ways and only half defeated a punch on the head by tripping over a bush and scrambling out of range.

"By God, I'll drown you for this," he panted.

"I'll—I'll—I'll—you wait," panted Sadie.

"You make me mad, the pair of you," wailed Pat. "I have me mind made up, I tell you. It's this. We're goin' off from here this minute. If you come after us I'll give her best to come at you and finish you for good."

He tossed Sadie off her feet and made off with her, and Carrol, with an exhausted gesture at this madhouse, prepared to follow. . . .

All that passed Gibble's addled mind without sentient proposals. He was conscious of nothing but a devastating hatred for that Irishman and ran crouching to take him in the rear. To Pat, this was Carrol that dodged behind him and he swung a punch which landed with divine precision on a human face.

Gibble found himself on all fours to a crashing impact of light and a ton weight balanced on his nose. He was scrambling blindly for something with his hands and found it. Pat saw Carrol before him still upright, and paused, confounded. He did not see Gibble rise stealthily behind him, clutching the lump of coral. His skull took the release of Gibble's fury and the earth was blacked out for him, and his joints collapsed and he went down at Sadie's feet, leaving her standing within the circle of his arms.

No one knew what had happened, Gibble least of all. He stood with the lump of coral raised to strike again, and lowered it with a gasp. Carrol and Sadie stared at him amazed, unable to account for his presence there. Then they discovered what he had done and Sadie stepped swiftly from Pat's body with a shiver.

It lay very still, keeping the crumpled posture of its fall, and its effect was to paralyse initiative in them. Carrol bent down to look closer and rose again. He put out a hand to touch the body and drew it back. After another tussle with repugnance he knelt down to peer at the head, listen at the lips and place a gingerly hand under the heart.

From that he rose hurriedly with a confounded expression.

"Damn it, he's dead."

"Dead?" repeated Sadie.

They stared at each other, unable to accept an incredible phenomenon.

Gibble had not attended to Carrol's investigation. He was concerned for a befogged sensation somewhere between the base of his skull and the bridge of his nose. He felt for that organ and located it in space. It seemed to distend outward a foot or so. At the same time he was aware of someone saying that the Irishman was dead, and was rushed by a violent need to reject an indecent utterance.

"He's not dead!   That can't be; that—that's impossible."

"See for yourself," said Carrol.

Gibble turned his head sharply away from the body.

"Not dead," he insisted angrily, backing towards the scrub.   "No, that's—that's——"

He turned abruptly and they heard him blundering through the brush towards the beach.   Carrol turned from that to look at Sadie, and at the body, and gave it up with an impatient sound.

"Damn these primitives, what the hell *can* you do with them?   Let's get out of this, Sadie, we can't do anything——"

He took her arm, anxious to get away from the vulgar arrogance of death, with its threat of inertia to the body and its detestable legacy of insincerity to the spirit.

They came out on the beach lost for a convention to restore life to its commonplaces.   One was waiting for them at the camp fire which they would willingly have dispensed with just then.   Gibble was crouched there on the sand with his face hidden and strangulated sobs jerking his shoulder blades, and Carrol's nerves nearly ejected an expletive at him. He dammed that up and they both stood there looking at Gibble, whose sobs became sensibly modulated, now that other ears were present. He made a dive at a phantom pocket, the decencies requiring a handkerchief just then. Lacking that he was forced to wipe a blurred vision of Carrol and Sadie into being by dabbing his eyes on his knees. His nose was vastly swollen, the indent of his brows puffed out and a shade of green had spread over both eyes. With a plaster of tears, it was a face sufficiently tragic.

"I never meant to do it," he exclaimed suddenly. "I no more thought of such a thing than—a fellow creature—struck down. Impossible! I couldn't do it. I had no knowledge even of—I only remember running in to help Sadie. He hit me—" Automatically he searched for his nose and found it. "Knocked me down. Then all I remember was——"

His attention lapsed there and he appeared to listen, investigating a remote outline of nose, unfamiliar, obtuse to contact but of a sensitivity recoiling from it. Gibble recoiled, to a burst of anger.

"He was dangerous; he had found that liquor. He knocked me about on the beach here. Violent. I knew that if he found Sadie—Then I heard him in there. Something had to be done. Consider what would have happened. A woman—helpless. He was a vile, dangerous brute. You know he was. You—" He located

Carrol, after a brief tussle with his nose. "If you hadn't been hiding in here it wouldn't have happened. He would have been alive now—a fellow creature. I knew something would happen, with all this secrecy going on. You wouldn't keep him in his place—force him to control himself. You encouraged him. And now, this—Something had to be done—something——"

"Yes, yes," said Carrol impatiently. "It's done, leave it at that. It's the only thing that could be done to the old blighter. The only real nuisance about it is that we'll have to bury him tomorrow, and I hate handling corpses."

"He was a fellow creature struck down without warning," exclaimed Gibble angrily. "And why? Because no one here made an effort to control themselves. All this loose talk. I said from the first, control him. Now it's too late. He had to be controlled, or else—You know what would have happened. He had Sadie at his mercy. My one thought was, save her."

Sadie's face made no concession to a noble motive for murder, nor did she reject it. Her eyes were calm and quite inscrutable as they stared at Gibble. Carrol shrugged and disposed of a need for justifications.

"Well, he's out of the road; let us accept that as a fact which explains itself."

"I won't be made responsible," exclaimed Gibble.

"Of course not; we were all in it."

"It was to save Sadie."

"Yes."

Gibble sank his chin on his knees, magnetized into

vacancy by an exploded emotion. The fire was dying down and Carrol placed more wood on it. In the kindling flame Gibble's eye was seen distended by a solemn thought.

"Dead!" he said.

"Yes."

"Struck down—ruthlessly."

"Yes. What did you hit him with?"

"A piece of coral. I found it here, at the camp."

"Oh, did you?"

"Fortunately, his back was towards me; otherwise I would have had no hope against him. He struck me a terrible blow. Terrible——"

He reached out in front of him, missed, and found his nose.

"For the moment I must have been almost unconscious. But by a powerful mental effort I——"

"Yes, yes.—Look here, don't you think we had better turn in?"

Gibble shook his head.

"Sleep would be impossible," he said. He also yawned.

"Well, I'm going. I feel damned used up."

"Sleep. No. Impossible," mumbled Gibble.

His head nodded. Carrol scratched his own, wondering vaguely why his mind rejected an effort to think coherently on a situation sufficiently coherent in drama. But just there Sadie uttered a cry of consternation and he turned swiftly. . . .

An apparition had joined them; the apparition of

Pat.　He stood in the outer range of firelight, swaying at the knees, turning on them the blank face of a corpse. Streaks of blood ran down his neck and chest and his hair was clogged with it.　Only his indomitable muscles held him upright and they were failing, and before Carrol could move he pitched forward on his face.

"Hell!" exclaimed Carrol, a cry that did not know it protested at an indecent anticlimax.　He ran to Pat and tugged him over to get his face out of the sand. The sticky slime of blood revolted him, but he managed to lever the body over and hold its head up.

"Get me a rag, Sadie, quick.　I must stop this bleeding."

Sadie's glare that had discovered Pat was still fixed on him, and Carrol had to repeat his demand for a rag and water before she detached her eyes with a frown to go without haste to the water breaker and fill a coconut shell.

"Rag—where's the rag?" said Carrol impatiently, but she shook her head obstinately.

"It's no use, I won't give up a single scrap of rag. You can tear a bit off your trousers if you must have it."

In a temper Carrol ripped one trouser leg off at the knee and tore it into strips.　He worked with haste to get a distasteful job done with, washing a jagged wound on the scalp and binding down a pad of rag to stop its bleeding.

Gibble had watched all that with a perfectly glazed

eye. Now he leaped up and clambered over to peer into Pat's face.

"Not dead!" he exclaimed.

He gripped Carrol's arm, demanding attention to an incredible oversight somewhere.

"He's not dead—not dead at all."

"Oh, go to hell," said Carrol, thrusting him off.

He finished binding the wound and was busy awhile making up a bed of bracken and lugging Pat onto it, with Gibble's rolled-up coat under his head. Sadie made no offer to help him, but stood by, lost in a brooding meditation.

"About all I can do," said Carrol. "Fancy the old devil walking here after that crack on the nut. But he's indestructible, of course."

He glanced round to discover that Gibble had vanished and added:

"Where's the murderer gone?"

Sadie gave an indifferent nod at the headland, which Carrol endorsed.

"Hope he stays there. He might want to explain why he failed to wipe out Pat."

"A pity Pat didn't settle him."

It was said without resentment, as comment on a piece of bungling to be expected. Carrol watched her go slowly across to the hut, where she now slept, and vanish into it. From that he fell to scratching his head and rubbing his neck and yawning, and exercise of protective vacuity which detached him from investigating the commonplace that man is a creature outside the functioning of a sentient process.

"I give this up; the blasted situation is hopeless," he muttered, crawling into his lair.

CHAPTER SEVENTEEN

CARROL awoke to sounds gruntulous and incredulous and came out to discover Pat sitting up and fingering his bandaged head.

"I've come by a thump somehow," he said in voice mild, and depleted of resonance.

"Yes, nothing to bother about, a mere flick of summer lightning. How do you feel on it?"

"Rotten. I have a drouth on me."

Carrol went over to pour him water, but he waved it peevishly aside.

"It's no use at all, it's a sup of liquor I need. Get me the bottle; I've a mind I left a fair-sized sup there for the morning."

"Where is it?"

"In the cave, of course, where you hid it on me."

His eyes were haggard and his hands shook, and Carrol went, noticing that Gibble was not in his lair.

241

He was lurking behind the headland and Carrol saw his head swiftly withdrawn behind a rock. From that an interval of meditation allowed him to emerge again, eyeing Carrol's approach with a certain apprehension.

"Is he—how is he?" he asked, craning at the camp.

"Quite alive, thanks."

Gibble sat down suddenly, in a pose of exhaustion.

"I've had a frightful night—frightful. No sleep. Just consider my——"

Carrol dived into the cave and retrieved the bottle. There was still liquor in it and he got off with it, though Gibble would have detained him to hear of an altruist's martyrdom.

"Give it here," exclaimed Pat, and took a swig with trembling haste. It revived him vastly, and he sat smacking his lips and respiring gratefully.

"Grand stuff," said he.

"Grand. I don't wonder you've got a head on you all the same. You got through something over a quart of it yesterday."

"I'd take the like of that a week on end without noticin' it. It's the crack on the head that sets me flitterin'. What was it you hit me with?"

"I didn't hit you; your little friend Gibby did that."

"Never tell me," said Pat, astonished. He was also pleased, by the way he felt his wound, as a distinction bizarrely acquired. "A fair-sized welt," he said approvingly. "I never thought he had it in him to hit a blow the weight of that."

Sadie came out of the hut and with a glance at Pat

that ignored him, went off to her rock pool to wash. She came back austerely and commenced to grill fish. Gibble had come lurking round the headland, and now a gracious odour of cooked food took a pull at his umbilicus, though he approached gingerly, with an apprehensive eye on Pat, in spite of the reassuring debility of his bandaged head.

"Come here now, and let me have a look at you," called Pat.

He found this command finely rewarded when Gibble's bunged nose and now prismatically coloured eyes were presented for inspection.

"Never say I done that on you," he said, astonished. It was the eye of a connoisseur that marked this facial disaster and accounted it a work finely executed.

"A fair likely punch it was. I had it in me mind I hit someone. The pair of us is even on it. Shake hands now."

Gibble reluctantly advanced a hand, which was handsomely shaken. The ceremony appeared to relieve him immensely.

"I can assure you I had no intention of hitting you like that," he said solemnly.

"Of course, you had. It's hot blood made you do it. You have a temper in you when roused."

"I fear I have, Pat."

"Devil a lie in it, you have the makin's of a hell of a feller with a bit of proper handlin'. Sit down here and let you and me have a talk together. What was it you hit me with?"

"A—er—a piece of—er—rock."

"A likely lump it was, by the feel. The wonder is you got in on me so quick after the punch I give you. Not many would come at it again on the top of that, and there's where your temper come in. Did I ever tell you———"

"Eat your food," said Sadie peremptorily.

All reached obediently for their platters of bark, Pat and Gibble eating side by side in a now established intimacy. Carrol was forced to eat with discretion, because there was something extremely ludicrous and annoying in that fraternity of damaged heads. But Sadie's eye altogether rejected it as a desirable grouping. Whatever her meditations may have been over a theory of surbordination versus a threat of anarchy, this peaceful aftermath to its uproars got no approval from her. Pat's air to Gibble was at once patronizing and flattering; the master now aware of zeal and worth in a disciple, and to fulsome exchanges in those terms Sadie's eyes opened wide, and remained open. When Pat, having eaten, stretched himself at ease to say heartily, "Did I ever tell you, Gibby, how me and a queer feller called Ginger Conklin had the horrors together at Oporto?" her eyebrows had reached their zenith.

"And you won't, either," she said. "There's been quite enough time wasted sitting about listening to your gabble. Look at that hut. Not a stroke done on it since the last rain. Now I'll tell you what you'll do. You'll put another layer of grass all over the

roof and make it completely water-tight. Then you'll make a decent bed in it and other things. I don't suppose there's anything in that bark cloth rot, but you can try it. Coverings of some sort must be made. Then a bonfire has got to be built in case of ships. As for *you*—" which was Pat, "you've had all the drink that there is to be had, and that's the end of another silly exhibition like last night. You won't try that sort of thing on again, I can tell you. As for *you*—" that was Gibble, "you'll take charge of the fishing and the fire again, and if you try any more of your sulking following about tricks you'll be sorry for it. As for *you*—" (Carrol) "you'll take charge of the fruit, and when you've done that, you'll spend two hours cutting bushes to make that bonfire."

She stamped. "What are you all sitting gaping at me for? Get up and do as you're told at once."

All rose, including Pat. To him Sadie said peremptorily, "Sit down. You can spend your time stripping grass till your idiotic head's better."

Pat sat. Gibble and Carrol went off about their duties with a marked effect of business urgency, very different from their usual manner of drifting through a job. Carrol was indignant at being addressed in that crude way as "you," which failed completely to distinguish him from the "yous" addressed to Pat and Gibble. But he made his round to the fruit-bearing trees and came back to camp for the axe, and put in a period of hard work, cutting down greenstuff and dragging it up to the headland. He was taking a well-earned rest on the pile when Sadie came across to her beach for the morning swim, and she stopped to cast an overseer's eye at the result of his labour.

"Call that a decent morning's work?" she said scornfully, and Carrol snatched up the axe in a temper and went back to slash it out of the bushes.

He spent the afternoon finishing the chair he had begun a week back, while Gibble thatched and Pat twisted fibres to bind the chair. Its seat and back were made of interlaced fibres bound to the frame, and it was a very creditable job, in Carrol's opinion, but Sadie only examined it carefully, tested it, and said, "Put it in the hut. You can go on with the bed tomorrow."

On those terms order was maintained. None of them questioned the process till it was established, because Sadie maintained a firm attitude of rejecting discussion on either its methods or their results. She had fearful powers of silence and exercised them ruthlessly, and their effect was to dispose of social ease in her presence. It is not to be supposed that she formulated any theory of establishing a feminine despotism, she merely submitted to annoyance over three irresponsible idiots of men and took it out of them on a well-approved method.

As a result, it divided the male population of the island into two factions, Carrol being one and Pat and Gibble the other.

Those two were much together, when duties permitted, and the tone of their exchanges was one of

unctuous conspiracy from Pat and a darkling concession to it from Gibble.

Gibble remained the factor of disruption in the group because he was genuinely disrupted. He partly repressed exhibitions of brooding in Sadie's presence, but he did a great deal of it in private. Forever he was tortured by the vision of a perfect love affair suspended in space, and the only outlet for its dammed-up emotion was to announce an awful wrong done him, and that was frustrated for lack of present evidence. Sadie made no more of Carrol than himself or Pat, though he watched incessantly for signals of treachery. He probably hated Carrol a great deal more for failing to provide them than for being the original cause of them, such was his need to explode repressions, and he had a master prompter to frenzy at his elbow. . . .

He came out of the bush from wood getting with Pat as Carrol passed into it going for fruit. He ignored them, and they watched him as lurchers in a back slum resent an intruding alien.

"He's a funny feller and all," said Pat. "Will you tell me if you've made up your mind he's had her or not."

"No," said Gibble scowling.

"Reason is for saying he has, if the eye is at fault catchin' him at it. It's my opinion he had her."

"How do you know?" demanded Gibble violently.

"It's by brain work I have the opinion. For why is it with nothin' doin' the pair is to be seen at any time not doin' it? With somethin' doin', not a squint

have I come by of them doin' it. Is it reason to say
they'd be that cunnin' for nothin'?"

Gibble hurled down his wood and scowled at it, and
at Pat, and at the direction gone by Carrol, and Pat
marked him with approval.

"And that's the way they puts it over you," said he.
"Face to face and man to man I put it to him he
has her and he gives me his word he has not. A liar
he is, from the feet up. It's my opinion you should
give him a punch in the slats to put him wrong with
the girl and put yourself right with her. Isn't he forever callin' you a ditherin' runt and worse behind your
back? It's not the thing a feller with hot blood under
his hat the like of you would put with. Never have
it said of you, Gibby lad, you give him his way to have
the laugh of you."

Gibble snatched up his load with white dents playing
like summer lightning about a scarlet face, and was
led to the camp to a soothing incitement to frenzy,
where he got into trouble by hurling his wood down
and scattering it all over the cooking place.

"Oh, indeed!" said Sadie, which was sufficient, for
Gibble collected the wood and put the pile in order,
though his compressions were not relieved by the act
of submission. Sadie waited till it was done and said
coldly:

"You can go on with the bed till Jimmy gets back.
You (Pat) go on with that bark."

She returned to her chair in the hut's doorway and
resumed her knitting. Carrol had shaped and scraped

smooth a pair of knitting needles and she was very intent on experimenting with grasses and fibres as material for woven fabrics. The interior of the hut was now neatly in order. The walls were lined with palm leaves interlacing upright sticks. Her wardrobe was a species of meat safe on four legs, lined with bark. In it were neatly folded her dress, pants, stockings, and every piece of cloth that could be extorted from the others. Trousers were all that remained to them. Even Pat's bandages had been demanded back as his wound healed, and had been carefully washed and stowed away. Her polished cigarette case served as a mirror. Below it was a shelf for her comb and rings and bracelets. The fan was attached to the wall as a decoration. Coconut bowls were filled with water and flowers placed in them daily. Now only the bed and its coverings remained to be completed. . . .

An effect of ordered existence in these matters was extremely pleasing to Sadie. It became her central preoccupation, which sufficed her for a motive in seeing that its services were performed.

Down by the lagoon Pat was tapping away at a large sheet of banyan bark spread out on a smoothed tree trunk. He tapped with a flat baton of wood, but hardly with inspiring results. The art of pulping it flat without knocking holes in it was not yet theirs but they were kept at it by relays and were very bored with it.

Gibble worked at the bed, which was a frame on legs lashed with fibre. They were now about its substitute for a wire mattress, which was to interlace strands of

fibre lashed to the frame.   It was a job requiring two
workers, and Gibble kept hopping from one end to
the other with the over-activity of a man in a bad
temper. . . .

Carrol was late back from fruit gathering.   In fact,
he had been submitting to his vice of practicing isolation in his bolt-hole.   He sneaked hours off there when
he couldn't stand any more of Gibble's presence just
then, and Sadie had a certain way of looking at him
after one of these absences which accounted them
marked as derelictions of duty.   But with his eyes half
closed against the sky's hypnotism, and walled in by his
little sanctuary, he was able to arrive at the false calm
of nihilism.

". . . No matter, things have got to go to pot in the
end, that's inevitable.   Of course, I see her drift, even
if she doesn't.   Keep all at an equal distance from her
and no one can demand a special privilege.   All very
well at present but how is it going to work when the
signs begin to show?   Gibble will go clean demented
and Pat will egg him on.   Well, that's a combination
outside my powers.   Curse that bloody Gibble, he's the
snag that's going to upset the whole thing.   If I could
make a combination with him it might be possible to
keep Pat in order, but there's no chance of that.   No
use talking to Sadie about it, either.   She won't hear
of my notion of at least trying to talk Gibble over . . ."

Talk!

Carrol was an intelligent fellow; much too intelligent
to discover that his rationality over Sadie was due to

the simple fact that he had possessed her. But Sadie's rationality went one better than that by quite dispossessing herself of Carrol. When he got back with his fruit that afternoon she gave him a hard glance and said:

"Don't pretend you've been all this time getting fruit."

"Well, no. The fact is I sat down to rest and went to sleep——"

"Go and help with that bed; it needs two to tie the ends properly."

Carrol went, fuming at a job with the detested Gibble. They refused to look at each other, working with speed in an awful silence. When one fumbled at a tying the other could hardly contain himself at such bungling, and there was much snatching at ends passed from one to the other. . . .

Carrol tugged his end viciously and jerked it out of Gibble's hand. He had done that before and now jerked a furious protest out of Gibble too.

"You did that on purpose."

"Rot!"

"You did. Tugged it out of my hand."

"Pass that end and shut up."

Corked up to bursting point, Gibble passed it and Carrol pulled it so sharply from him that he fell against the frame.

"Clumsy cow," exclaimed Carrol.

Gibble swiped a blow at him and missed. They grappled and went down in an explosion of punches, with Carrol underneath, hissing expletives and getting home with effect on Gibble's ribs. His one burning obsession was to punch Gibble's still tender conk; Gibble defeated that by applying throttling tactics. . . .

Pat threw down his baton and came leaping with glad outcries. He shouted encouragement as he ran. Sadie put down her knitting and came hurrying too. She grabbed Gibble by the neck and pulled him over on his back. When he scrambled up she slapped his face hard and he went down again. By that time Carrol was on his feet and she pushed him back.

"I thought I could trust you to have a little sense!" she exclaimed furiously. "Get out of this at once."

Carrol breathed in his rage, noted Gibble still on the ground, and walked off. Sadie turned on Pat and Pat turned at once and went back to his tapping.

She stood over Gibble, studying him with a lowering brow. The white print of her slap still showed clearly on his pink skin and he sat there confused, and unable to meet her eyes. Sadie matured an opinion on him but did not utter it. She only said, "Go on with that bed," and walked back to her chair.

Gibble returned to his job, working at it in a chastened spirit, which had forgotten Carrol. That slap on the face from her still confused him, for it rejected him by rushing on him a charmed image of abasement to her. Now he was confounded at his arrogance in thinking he could make a claim to command her.

When he glanced up to find her eyes fixed on him steadily over her knitting he looked away at once, more confused than ever.

CHAPTER EIGHTEEN

GIBBLE chose his opportunity, or thought he did. He had gone stripping palm leaf fibres in a glade well away from the camp where Pat and Carrol were working. But Sadie had gone strolling that way too, knitting as she dawdled here and there among the bushes. Presently she sat down to spread the fabric over her knees and study it.

Gibble came awkwardly across to her, expecting a command to go on with his work, but Sadie said quite amiably:

"Not so bad, is it? When it's been wet and kneaded up it becomes much softer."

It was the first time she had spoken to him in that tone since the episode of his ruined love. Gibble dropped on his knees beside her, imploring concern for an awful uprush of self-pity.

"Why do you treat me like this?"

"Like what?"

"You know—always cold—distant. I can't bear it any longer. I'll go mad. One can't go on like this, never thinking of anything else. Never for a minute— a second. I love you. You must be kind to me."

He took her in a fragile embrace fearful of being repelled but Sadie only frowned a little, shaking her head.

"No, Gibby, I can't trust you. You know how you went on before."

"I know; I was vile, loathsome. Forgive me, Sadie. If you knew what I have suffered. I implore you, Sadie, forgive me. I don't care how little you love me; I don't care if you tread on me. Anything but this awful coldness. You must let me love you or I will go mad. Sadie, forgive me, forgive me. . . ."

Sadie forgave him. At least, she relaxed in his arms with a slightly distrait air, as if she were thinking about something else, which permitted her to overlook Gibble's now inspired ardour. He kissed her brow, her eyes, her lips, blown up with wonder at a divine concession. It rushed upon him as an incredible discovery that she was his—his. . . .

Well, perhaps she was, in theory. And theory may concede something to practice, if you catch it on the hop. Or if it catches you. Gibble lost his head at that point, which does away with a proposal to chronicle

imageries of phrenetic lyricism. Sadie put herself out
of action by closing her eyes with a slightly pained
air. . . .

But they were opened wide enough an hour later,
and their expression was very serious. So was Gibble's; there was even a hint of alarm in it.

"But, Sadie, surely—"

"No, Gibby, this has been madness. It must never occur again. I can't think why I took such a terrible risk. Just consider what a frightful thing it would be if——"

"My darling, we must trust that Providence——"

"No, Gibby, I refuse to trust to any such thing. It must never occur again, never."

"Your word is law," said Gibble reverently.

Carrol resented so strongly looking at Gibble that it was some time before he was forced to note a marked change of demeanour in their malcontent. For one thing, Gibble was now the busiest and most earnest worker on the island. His alacrity for service was conscious with Christian endeavour. He did not approach Carrol, but seemed to invite an approach from him. To Pat he was now distant and when approached for conversation had other matters to attend to. With Sadie, his manner was deferential to obsequiousness. . . .

But as Carrol still sulked, Sadie had a few serious words with him in private about it. "I've spoken to Gibby and he has promised to cause no more trouble, and the least you can do is to be decent too, and stop this constant scowling about the camp."

A week later she had a few serious words with Gibble in private too, and they blenched even his irresponsible pinkness. He came back to camp with his eye fixed in alarm, and his deference to Carrol seemed to propitiate an unadmitted calamity too. Pat, professional observer of other people's affairs, sought out Carrol to comment on it.

"What's come over the queer feller to make him so meek these days? He has a look of a man who has a burr in his bottom. It's my opinion she's put the strangle holt on him one way or another, but how she's done it I have me doubts for the minute."

"Oh, go and hide behind a bush and find out," said Carrol dyspeptically.

Inspection on any terms failed to detect Sadie in a private grouping of two. She maintained her state in public, but her austerity had now relented, and she permitted her voice a tone of social concession at meal times. The daily routine of work was resumed, but she had also set them a job building a hut for themselves, pointing out that she couldn't have them in hers every time it rained.

A strong easterly gale had blown all that day, with storms of rain, and they had been forced to shelter in the hut and sleep there too. This had quite disordered that neat place, making a mess of it with piles of bracken, and Sadie was very firm about making a provision against that sort of nuisance again. "You'll begin it this afternoon," she said.

The axe dictated exchanges of labour. Gibble required it for wood cutting while Pat and Carrol were away after fruit, and Carrol took it over when he returned for bonfire building. He had a fine pile on the headland. . . .

The sun came up on a freshly washed island, causing it to steam again, and Carrol to sweat as he dragged up boughs and pitched them up on the pile. He worked at that till he had earned a spell, and stopped to take it, watching the white-topped combers racing from the horizon under a blue sky.

Sadie passed below the headland to her beach, and he turned to watch her tall naked figure patterned against a shining strip of sand as she tossed off her rags and ran down to the water. How long would she be able to do that now before a scandal was abroad? It seemed months since its awful threat had been burst on him, and he knitted his brows to discover that was only three weeks ago.

"Oh, well, I give it up," he said as usual, without being able to give it up. He sat down by the pyre, submitting to interjections of thought on interludes of not thinking. Out of one he said:

"I wonder how she's got Gibble under."

An interval.

"Only one way, damn it."

Another.

"Hell, I wish the cow was implicated. All the same, I'd like to punch his nose if he is."

From a final vacuity he interjected

"But Pat—!"

He gave that up.

He gave up all speculation with a shock just then, because he discovered his eyes fixed on something at the sea rim. It came and went, wavering out of focus and back again, but persistent gazing insisted on a faint triangle alternately light and dark.

He sat there, aghast at a quandary that threatened

hope defeated. It might be worse defeated by an outcry that acclaimed it too soon, and he sat and sat in an
agony of suspense till that triangle was cleanly visible;
the topgallant sails of a ship.

Carrol scrambled and fell down to the cave and dived in, snatching for the matches. His hands trembled so he could hardly tear the covering from them. He grabbed up a mass of dried fibre in bolting back aloft, and butted it into the pile where the leaves were driest and struck a match. The fibre licked it up and the mass began to crackle, till the breeze whipped it to a broad flame which drove into the damper masses and began to vomit smoke.

Gibble and Pat ran out from the camp and stared, but at Carrol's yell, "A ship," they bolted madly for the headland. Sadie dived from the reef and swam a race against time to reach the beach, and ran naked to help. By that time Pat was slashing at the undergrowth with the axe while Gibble and Carrol dragged the hewn masses to the blaze and hove them on it. A fine column of smoke now poured up and over the island, but no one stopped working a moment. A cessation of labour might cause that lifting cone of white on the sea rim to sink again. . . .

It lifted steadily, from topsails to mainsails, drawing up the hull of a full-rigged ship; the last conquest by beauty left on sea.

For all their fears of hope defeated she came fast enough on a six-knot breeze, heading straight for the island. That was so incredible that they were still piling boughs on the fire when she hove to a quarter of a mile out with her foreyards aback. The white curve of a boat lifted on her quarter and was run out to drop neatly on the water. At that they all ran shouting to the lagoon, waving at the boat that dipped and rose across the swell towards the reef.

Sadie was the first to recover a rational poise in a now rational world. She dipped in the lagoon to wash off smudges from the fire and scampered up to the hut. Pat patrolled the beach, jaunty with military erectness. Carrol and Gibble were out on the reef, signalling the boat's course to the channel.

She came strongly in on the swell, rowed by four shock-heads in dungarees, and steered by a burly youth in a reefer cap, who stared with unaffected interest at the bright-eyed derelicts on the reef. They dived in to swim ashore with the boat, which was beached, and the youth in command compactly landed, to be welcomed as an ocean demigod.

"What astounding luck," burbled Carrol.

"Providential," breathed Gibble.

"Castaways, eh?" said the youth.

"Yes, we drifted here, from the *Minorca*. She was run down. Lord, I've lost count of time——"

"The third of August," said Gibble.

"The *Minorca*," said the youth. "I remember reading about that in Frisco. She was run down by an oil tank. There were four or five passengers missing. I thought one was a woman."

"Damn the lie in it, so she is, an' one was a fireman, and the smartest hand in the black pan watch at that," said Pat.

"Oh, you're the greaser, are you?" said the youth,

with a compactness that took in Pat at a glance and left him there.

"Quite right, there are four of us," said Carrol, glancing round for Sadie. "My name's Carrol, this is the Rev. Mr. Gibble."

"My name's Clegg," said the youth.

They shook hands formally. That is, Clegg shook hands with Carrol and Gibble. Then he stopped, stared, and put his cap straight. Sadie had finished her toilet and now emerged from the hut. She wore her evening frock, her silk stockings and kid shoes. Her hair was smoothly combed and plaited and her bracelets, rings and wristlet watch in place. The dress was of lemon-tinted crêpe de chine and made a distinguished harmony with her honey-coloured hair and skin. To a male eye she might have stepped off the *Minorca's* promenade deck five minutes ago. Even Carrol was astonished.

"Miss Sadie Patch," said he with aplomb.

Clegg was quite confounded and took off his cap twice while being introduced. The shock-heads behind goggled astonishment. With Carrol, Gibble and Pat naked but for a remnant of trouser, Sadie's stylish appearance raised strange questions on the economy of desert islands. But Sadie had other matters to think about.

"Are we going off from here at once?" she demanded.

"Well—I mean to say, what's the water like here? Good? That's good. Ours has gone stale. We were

certainly blown three points off our course by the gale
last night and the dam' fool—I beg your pardon, I
mean the bloody—I mean to say, jibed her up—lost
us our fore to'gallant mast and—we saw your fire, I
mean to say, after we put in here for water——"

"Pat, show these chaps where the water is," said
Carrol, coming to Clegg's assistance. There were casks
in the boat and Clegg was all adrift under Sadie's in-
flexible stare.

"You're not making excuses about not taking us off,
are you?" she demanded.

"Hell—I beg your pardon—no," protested Clegg.
"We saw your fire, of course, but there's no saying we
weren't blown off our course, losing that stick, but I
mean to say I'm bl— I mean to say, glad of it, as we
wouldn't have sighted this island and had the luck—I
mean to say the pleasure of taking you off."

"Oh, then that's all right," said Sadie.

"Yes," said Clegg, relieved. "You managed to
come away with a nice lot of clothes."

"Not a stitch but what I stand up in."

"Well, but how did you manage to keep that dress
so nice?" expostulated Clegg.

"I put it away and only used my petticoat and
singlet," said Sadie solemnly.

"Oh," said Clegg, relieved of a mystery.

"And where are we going after we leave here?"

"Sydney's our next port."

"Sydney. How long will it take to get there?"

"Well, that's a question. Depends on the wind

With any average luck we could do it in three or four
weeks. Perhaps less, perhaps more."

"What's the date now?"

"November the second."

Sadie made some rapid mental calculations and let
Clegg off a cross-examination that left him very much
more its subjective than its subject.

"I can assure you I'm extremely glad we lost that
stick," he told Carrol earnestly.

"By ginger, so am I," Carrol assured him.

In half an hour's time Clegg's water barrels were
full and a mass of fruit piled in the boat. Carrol and
Gibble put on their bedraggled coats, but Pat made a
point of leaving his singlet behind. "There'll be a
slop chest on the limejuicer yonder," he said to Carrol.

"Come on," called Sadie impatiently from the boat.
They ran down to it, but Gibble recollected something
and ran back round the beach to the headland.

"What on earth has he gone for?" said Sadie, indignant at squandering time in such a place, but Gibble excused that by galloping back with two pocketbooks, his
own and Carrol's.

"Thanks, Gibby, I clean forgot it," said Carrol
warmly.

"Don't mention it," said Gibble with equal warmth.

Much appeared to be forgotten just then, with these
two exchanging courtesies and Sadie perched in the
stern with Clegg, like a lady of fashion gone jaunting
out of season. But now they were off, and the smooth

passage of the boat driven outward on the swell recalled the process of their arrival there.

"This is a bit better than lumbering about in a boat
without oars," said Carrol.

"You were lucky; one chance in fifty of landing
anywhere," said Clegg.

"Be damned to that; wasn't I in the boat?" said
Pat. "Do you mind me sayin' it's my luck agen yours
and that was luck for the lot of us?"

"Yes, you were like the benevolence of God, we had
to put up with you," said Carrol.

Clegg approved of that, without saying so. He was
very busy just then, taking charge of Sadie, and explaining away a discrepancy in his ship's appearance by
the providential loss of that topgallant mast; very much
in the key of a host concerned to create an impression
on a distinguished guest.

". . . It carried away the bob stay as you can see and
that accounts for the stream chains set up through the
hawse-pipes. But we'll have that stick rigged in no
time . . ."

"I think she looks perfectly lovely."

"Well, she is; a kid could steer her——"

"Can she sail really fast?"

"You bet. She's done three hundred twenty miles
in twenty-four hours."

They came lifting and sinking on the swell alongside the stained grey hull to where a pilot ladder trailed
from the break of the poop, where heads looked curi-
ously down at them.

"Throw down a bowline, you," commanded Clegg, and when that was done he adjusted it under Sadie's arms, steadying her at the ladder.

"Catch hold above my hands as she rises; you'll be quite safe," he assured her.

She was, inclosed in Clegg's arms, which took possession of Sadie and the ladder together, and arrived on deck to a breathless acknowledgment of silk-stockinged legs, alow and aloft. Carrol and Gibble tumbled up after them and Pat came last, at leisure and at ease.

"Bos'n!" called Clegg.

The boatswain came across from a spare spar laid along the deck and Clegg jerked a thumb at Pat. "Take this man forrard," he said.

A masterly settlement of their main island complexity. Carrol had not time to admire it, because Captain Curran of the *Acanora* was waiting on the poop to be presented in form. He was a big sandy man with a clipped red brush of moustache, but he rejected opinion on a tough exterior by an amiable and cultivated voice, and he dawdled a little on his words, which he used sparingly.

"Delighted," he said, when Clegg had made their introductions. "The *Minorca*—well, well—congratulate myself . . ."

Clegg went forward, bawling orders. The boat was hoisting in and hands went to the braces. Captain Curran said politely, "A moment," and turned to the companionway, where the steward was staring with astonishment at the castaways. To him the Captain

gave a keyed-down instruction which the steward itemized by taking a mental measurement of Carrol and Gibble before darting down the companionway stairs. "This way," said Captain Curran, motioning his guests below.

The saloon gave them a rare sensation, with its green leather upholstery and white panelling, its silverware in sideboard racks and moreover, a cabinet gramophone, but Captain Curran's art of host made nothing of entertaining two almost defunct pairs of trousers and an ultra-stylish evening frock. There was a mirror there too, and Carrol studied himself aghast.

"God! What a frightful looking cow," he protested. "One of my nightmares was to wake up with whiskers and now it's happened."

But he forgot even that because the steward was setting out a tea tray on which were biscuits and buttered scones.

"Tea!" exclaimed Sadie.

They hasted to gather 'round a treat and Carrol, between mouthfuls, told what there was to tell of their island adventure. Surprising how little there was to tell, too, but perhaps that was understood, with Sadie present and Captain Curran a discreet and polite man.

"Well, well, you all look remarkably well on it," he said conventionally.

"All the same, it doesn't compensate," said Carrol. "The only really simple life you can lead is an unhealthy one in a large city."

Captain Curran filled their cups again and Sadie

took her sixth scone. "Nothing but fish and fruit to eat for months," she explained.

"These scones are really delicious," said Gibble solemnly.

"That reminds me, my hairpins," she said to Gibble.

"But we used them."

"Not all."

"There were two left, and we left them behind."

"We used them for fish-hooks," explained Carrol.

"If that isn't too bad," said Sadie, annoyed.

"Too bad, too bad," agreed Captain Curran.

"If you only knew the state my underwear is in," said Sadie, solemn with horror.

Captain Curran intimated politely that his imagination was at her service there. But he added incidentally, "Er—steward," and that zealous creature bent to be instructed in the ear and to haste on a secret mission.

In short, when Sadie was shown to her cabin she found displayed on its bunk a pair of silk pyjamas, a Chinese silk bathrobe, a very handsome shawl, a roll of linen and needles, cotton, scissors and a paper of hairpins; these of the carpenter's recent manufacture.

"Hope you'll manage to patch up something from these odds and ends," said Captain Curran, dawdling at the door.

Sadie ran impassioned fingers over each article, a devotee in the presence of sacred things. Reverence for a man of exalted vision was the stare that rewarded Captain Curran.

"Delighted," he murmured vaguely, and departed.

Carrol found shirts, socks, shoes and shaving materials, and the steward in attendance, like a dealer in second-hand clothes, with an assortment to try on.

"I thought Mr. Gadget would be about your size," he said, when a suit of Mr. Gadget's shoregoing togs had been selected. "Perhaps you'd better gimme the scissors, sir, I'm used to hair cutting."

He left Carrol barbered and lathering a face that now pleased him in the shaving mirror. It was bronzed and hardened and he indulged a little male vanity as he shaved, balancing himself against the gentle heeling of the ship. It recalled him suddenly to the consciousness of motion, and he thrust his face to the porthole, just in time. Away on the ship's quarter a miniature pattern of palms dwindled against the sky. Presently they were only a faint tracery lost and found between the waves and then had vanished behind a curve of ocean, sinking with them a dream of isolation.

CHAPTER NINETEEN

B Y NIGHTFALL they were at home on the *Acanora* and her saloon was the brightest place on earth, if one may apply that convention to the sea. Carrol and Captain Curran had surprised one of those pleasing intimacies which spring up ready-made, by some inflection of words that accept an exchange of ideas as understood. Carrol had done without communion in those terms for some time and welcomed it with gusto.

Clegg, but for Captain Curran's presence, would have deferred all precedence to Sadie and conferred all her attention on himself. As it was, the homage of an earnest seducer had to deport itself as a decorous first officer taking his watch off below. He was very struck. Sadie had braided her hair and manicured her hands and draped the Chinese robe into a charming dishabille. She was stitching a camisole, and her eyelids drooped contentedly over a world restored to underwear. When she raised them it was to meet Clegg's eyes, but that was because he sat just in front of her and watched her all the while.

Gibble sat on the settee beside her, seeking to intrude conversation between her and the respectful but obnoxious Clegg. He had retained his beard but the steward had cut his hair. The trousers supplied him were a little short, and that kept him making fidety adjustments between his socks and braces. The thing that disturbed him most was that in this unexpected setting Sadie seemed less approachable than before he had possessed her, and he was very muddled about the status of a perfect love affair, in either its rewards or its retributions. What he wanted to do was to get Sadie apart and have a long and earnest talk with her, but she never gave him a hint that there was now anything to talk about. . . .

"Quite sure you won't smoke?" said Captain Curran for the third time.

"No, thanks," said Carrol.

"You will, though."

"No fear. Why, I came through that business with one cigarette intact. I believe it's still in Sadie's case. One of the things I discovered over there was that the less you get out of life the better off you are."

He edged at the gramophone and away again. It was probably stored with rubbish, anyway.

"It's all rot, the notion that emotion defines a reaction to life. All it does is to exasperate a perception of it. Who wants to know a thing as rottenly obvious as life? The best times I had over there were lying on my back thinking of nothing. I was getting pretty good at it, too."

By that time he had opened the gramophone and was going through its records. They reflected the usual muddle between values in music and the virtuosity of its rendering, but there was some real music there and he picked out the Finale of *Götterdämmerung* and vacillated over it.

"I've foresworn this poison, all the same," he said, setting the disc revolving. All the same, the first bars caused him to hold his breath and he leaned forward, fearful of missing a modulation. . . .

"Fine thing," said Captain Curran conventionally, as the music ended. He pushed over the cigarette box and Carrol took one and lit it before Captain Curran's grin apprised him of the act.

"Oh, well, I don't care," he said. "I don't suppose there's any escape from the system. But tell me, Captain, did you make a note of the bearings of that island? I mean so that it could be found again?"

"Yes. You didn't leave any buried treasure there, did you?"

"I did. Some day I may want to go back and dig it up. I believe that life might be nearly perfect alone on a desert island with a dog and a gramophone."

"Jimmy Carrol, you are quite mad," said Sadie.

But Carrol was again going through the records and Clegg couldn't stand that bloody awful music, and he rose, saying carelessly to Sadie, "Lovely night; perhaps you'd like to take a turn on deck."

Sadie put down her sewing and went with him at once, leaving Gibble alarmed. Captain Curran signalled to the steward, who brought whisky and glasses. This was pleasant, and Carrol filled his glass. "Mr. Gibble?" said the Captain, offering the bottle.

"Er, no, no, thanks," said Gibble hurriedly. "In fact, I—er—think I'll take a turn on deck."

He went, and Carrol said indiscreetly, "Hallo, Gibby's got it bad again."

Captain Curran was too polite to press inquiry on a cryptic utterance but his eye did so. Carrol pulled up his chair with a glance at the companionway. The opportunity for a little intellectual scandal was not to be resisted.   Besides, he urgently needed to tell someone what he thought of Gibble.

"Well, here's luck, Captain.   You know, that jaunt of ours over there wasn't at all as simple as it may look at present.   Not by a long chalk.   In fact . . ."

Surprising what a lot there was to tell about their island adventure.   Carrol had to shut up suddenly an hour later when Sadie came downstairs, blinking a little at the light.   Clegg followed her.   Gibble followed Clegg, and there was a faint inflection of dents on a general austere pinkness.   Carrol and Captain Curran very carefully refrained from glances confessing the practice of indiscreet psychology.

But for that matter, Carrol was as uncertain as Gibble of where the suspense factor of their island grouping had got to, though unlike Gibble, he was not very anxious to find out.   He took a well-earned rest from it.   Perhaps Sadie did too.   The wind was steady and they kept a course for Sydney, and Clegg took great pride in showing what the ship could do because Sadie so admired her sailing powers.   She went every day with him to mark their position on the chart and compute the distance gained. Once they ran into a heavy easterly gale, and Sadie spent the day on deck, in a suit of oilskins, for Clegg kept the *Acanora* under topgallant sails, and she drove with her lee rail under water and the spray flew over her poop like rain.   Carrol lay below, wedged into his bunk trying to read and not liking the experience at all.   Sadie's confessed terror of storms on the island was clearly a substitution for

interested in them. Worst of all, perhaps she was really interested in Clegg.

Carrol failed to see where any combination of Sadie with another could affect their still suspended island episode. He practised nihilism by refusing to think about it while constantly thinking about it.

CHAPTER TWENTY

C ARROL leaned on the poop rail, absorbing
the serenity of sailing under a summer night
of stars.

This easy motion of the ship might have done with
storm and stress for ever. The steersman's face, illu-
minated from below by the binnacle lamp, was that
of a mildly bearded demon, controlling the spokes of
a benign destiny. Light from the fluted glass of the
saloon skylight picked up the curve of the spanker, to
be lost in a cool radiance of stars. To let the eye
dwindle aloft by tiers of canvas to the swaying trucks
was to arrive by those pointers at the narcotic depth

284

of space and its idle pinpoints, the foolish unmeaning stars.

Below on the deck a cluster of pipes glowed as lesser constellations about the galley door. Pat was installed there, to make a light diversion of peeling potatoes and scrubbing saucepans while entertaining himself in the character of a professional raconteur. If by day he cocked a tolerant eye up at the poop it was to assure the others that he was in the joke about caste divisions on shipboard. Clegg detested him, detecting an insubordinate at a glance.

Clegg came along the deck now to submerge the glow of pipes in sounds of gruntulous haulage at the topsail halliards. He fussed about down there till no further exercises could be devised against a reglowing of pipes about the galley doors, and came aft to shoot his compact bulk up the poop ladder beside Carrol.

"I wish that greaser of yours was signed on," he said with venom. "Liverpool packet rat—I'd like to handle him a bit."

"I'd like to see you do it. He needs regular handling with a brick, or a shotgun."

"You had trouble with him over there, I bet."

"Yes. But we had some luck in return. A tree fell on him one time and a lump of rock——"

"No, how was that?"

Clegg suffered a lickerish curiosity for details of their island affairs. Perhaps he was afflicted by pre-present grouping jealousy, or perhaps he wanted to find out what happened when there were three men to one girl with a view to applying its theory to one girl and himself. Carrol allowed himself to be pumped with discretion in Clegg's case. He got out of the main difficulty of these disclosures by presenting Sadie as a grand dominant commanding strict submission from three vassals. One assumed from Carrol's viewpoint that he merely stood about and looked on at the whole business. By keeping himself out of the picture he was able to put its disgraces on Pat and Gibble, and made a good story of their coming to blows over Sadie and her slave-driving tactics in reprisal.

"Wonderful girl, that," said Clegg reverently. "Mind you, that's the sort that *can* love, once they let themselves go. I mean to say, given the right man . . ."

Sadie and Captain Curran emerged from the companionway for an after-dinner promenade. A moment later Gibble's head appeared and he looked at them, but as usual his meditations of approach failed at the august saunterings of Captain Curran on his own poop. A glance at Clegg and Carrol at the lee mizzen rigging sent him to the weather rail, where he brooded at the water below. The brief burst of graciousness between himself and Carrol had lapsed. Clegg had quite displaced Carrol as the intrusive factor on a perfect love affair, but he now suspected Carrol of talking about him to Captain Curran, and he deeply resented those groupings over the whisky of an evening. He badly needed something to resent just then, with the repressions of a perfect love affair fermenting within him. . . .

Clegg strolled to the binnacle and glanced from that to the weather leech of the royals. He was hoping that Captain Curran's saunterings would arrest themselves at Carrol and give him the chance of a few words with Sadie before he went off duty. Even so, there was that cock-eared slab of a parson waiting to butt in as usual. Clegg's wooing had been incessantly haunted by him. Carrol was a good fellow, even if he did talk through his hat at times, but that parson was beyond bearing. He needed a lesson, such as say, being picked up in the slack of the main brace; a nice clean run through the poop entrance overboard. Easy enough to pick the blighter up afterwards . . .

But Sadie had brought Captain Curran to arrest before Carrol to tell him something.

"Captain Curran says that if this wind holds we should be in Sydney within four days."

"Four days?"

"Sorry to lose you all, I'm sure," said Captain Curran.

He gave Carrol a faint inflection of one eyebrow, because Carrol had said to him the night before, "I'm hanged if I know what's in Sadie's mind about this business, and I wish she'd let it out, and of course I'll do anything she wants, naturally." Captain Curran had endorsed that—any sailor would. And Sadie was now tapping her teeth reflectively and opening her eyes at Carrol.

"I suppose you've arranged what to do about breaking the glad news to your people, Sadie," said Carrol.

"One thing I won't have is my people crowding down on us and my sister Fanny making an ass of herself all over the place. I suppose you *could* put us ashore without anyone knowing, Captain Curran."

"Well, yes, perhaps. A little difficult to keep an interesting event like this dark——"

"Oh, I only meant before they have time to find out we're on board."

"Of course, that will be simple."

Clegg struck eight bells, to his own annoyance, and Gadget came up the poop ladder. Resigning Sadie, Clegg went below. Captain Curran murmured a nothing and moved across to Gadget, with whom he discussed a darkening patch of sky to windward. The ship was heeling now as the wind strengthened and Gadget went forward to take in the royals. Gibble still leaned on the weather rail, staring darkly on the water, and Captain Curran slipped unobtrusively down the companionway.

With one impulse, Carrol and Sadie turned to the rail, leaning on it elbow to elbow.

"Now, Jimmy Carrol, what's to be done about this business?"

"Well, what *can* be done about it, Sadie?"

Sadie thought a moment before replying precisely:

"There's *one* way out of it, and that is that you can marry me the moment we get ashore."

Carrol suppressed a thrill of funk for another emotion which refused to label itself.   Consciousness of
worth in Sadie's estimation, perhaps. His voice dropped
to an earnest inflection as he asked:

"Do you want to marry me, Sadie?"

"No, Jimmy Carrol, I do not."

A crescendo of generous emotion on Sadie's behalf
went suddenly flat.

"You don't."

"I don't."

"Oh."

"No."

Carrol scowled but Sadie failed to notice it.

"A rotten idea, anyway, dashing ashore to get married and putting the whole show away on the spot."

"Then why the deuce did you propose it?"

"I didn't; I only said it was one way."

"What's the other?"

"Pretending we're going to get married and then
getting it fixed up."

"Is there time?   I'm infernally muddled about
dates."

"There'll be three weeks to spare if we get in as
Captain Curran says."

"Oh, then that's simple."

"Is it simple?"

"Why, you haven't got any scruples about it, have
you?"

"Of course, I haven't.   I don't believe in having
illegitimates—it's as rotten for them as for us.   And I

certainly don't want one forced on me the way this was."

"Oh, hell, don't start blaming me at this date."

"It was your fault."

"All right, it was. And I'll see you through the business. There's nothing to worry about."

"Isn't there? How am I to arrive home and kiss them all round and then disappear for a week without telling anyone where I'm going?"

"Hell, I never thought of that."

"That's why you've got to come home engaged to me, so that you can make an excuse to get me away for a week."

"What on earth sort of excuse?"

"Oh, you can say your people in Melbourne are just on the point of sailing for Europe and you want them to meet me before they sail. I'll have to let young Fanny into the know and we can take her with us in the car to make it look all right. We'll have to go by car in case they insist in seeing us off at the train. Then you can run me straight to wherever I've got to go to get fixed up and clear off to post my letters back from Melbourne. I did it for the little wretch once and now she can do it for me."

"H'm, sounds workable. I'd have to lie low for the week too, because my people are in Sydney. I wish to God we could defer our official arrival home for one week."

"Well, it can't be helped. Your people don't know my people and there won't be any difficulty with them as long as it's understood we're engaged to be married."

"Married! ! !"

They whipped round at a furious protest behind them. Gibble stood there. He had come across in his canvas shoes because he could not bear that prolonged secret conference any longer. One word caught had exploded its awful treachery.

"Sadie, what's the meaning of this? I insist on knowing."

"Lower your voice," exclaimed Sadie.

"You said 'married.' I heard you. You can't marry 'im."

"Oh, indeed."

"You can't, and you know why."

"You mind your own business."

"I won't endure this. You are my wife in the sight of God. If you don't tell him the truth I will."

"Will you shut up?" exclaimed Sadie, but Carrol had uttered an angry expression of enlightenment.

"Ho! So this cow was in it too."

"You dare—" stammered Gibble, "you dare make such a claim."

"Oh, dry up. You only came in at the tail end of it."

Gibble snatched a grip at Carrol who shoved him off. Sadie made a furious gesture at both of them, hissing, "You dare make a scandal here."

It stopped them, and Sadie jammed her clenched fists to her ears, shutting out a male bedlam in order to

think in it.   Then she drew a deep breath and turned
on Gibble:

"You—you pestilent creature!   If it hadn't been
for you——"

Her venom left Gibble aghast.   From him she
turned on Carrol.

"You're a bright intelligent fellow, aren't you, not
to see the truth under your nose?   Of course, he was
in it.   What other way was there of keeping him out
of it?   And if you had had a spark of decent self-
control there wouldn't have been any need for him.
How was I to know we were going to get away from
that island?   I thought I had years of you idiots to
face there and a kid on top of it.   You had a sample
of the way those two were going on, and the only way
to keep them quiet was the way you were kept quiet."

"Them!" ejaculated Carrol.

"Of course, Pat had to be brought in too.   Do you
think I was fool enough to leave him out?   I hope that
hurts your feelings.   It was this imbecile who forced
Pat on me and it was you who forced him on me.   And
I tell you flatly I needed Pat more than either of you,
for if I couldn't control you I intended to turn him on
you.   If I had to have a kid I was going to see that it
had some sort of protection."

Carrol leaned sullenly on the rail, convicted of nothing to say.   But Gibble stood with a working face, com-
prehending only one last vast iniquity to all his in-
justices.

"That Irishman!   You let that——"

Sadie slapped his face viciously.

"Get out of my sight. It was you who made the whole thing a nightmare. I don't mind Pat, but I detest myself when I think of you."

But that slap released an unbearable mechanism in Gibble. He saw everything lost that only an act of abasement might have retained, and slumped suddenly on his knees, gripping Sadie round the legs.

"Forgive me—I don't care what—you must take me——"

A heavy gust canted the ship and Sadie grasped at the rail, impeded by Gibble's clutch. From forward came Gadget's shout, "T'gallant halliards," and the yards rattled down to a howling cry at the weather braces. Hands came on the poop to let go halliards and go aloft by the weather rigging.

Sadie was tugging furiously at Gibble. "Make him stand up," she hissed at Carrol.

They lugged him up and hung him over the rail, where Sadie held him with a policeman's grip.

"You dare make a scene here," was all she said.

But potency had gone out of Gibble. He came away from the rail with a stagger, grabbed at the poop ladder railing and went down at a rush. A moment later they heard the door at the poop alleyway clatter open and bang shut.

To the trampling of the watch coming aft to take in the mizzen topgallant Carrol said bitterly:

"I give in to all you say about that damned situation, Sadie, and I admit that you did the only possible thing in making everyone equally responsible for it, but hang it, you needn't have lumped me in with those other two. I did the best I could for you."

"Yes, and what *could* you do?"

She shrugged that off to add:

"To think of having an idiotic scene like this forced on me after all the other business. But I'll watch that fool till we land. If he dares make a fuss . . ."

CHAPTER TWENTY-ONE

THE *Acanora's* gig pulled in to the stairway of a Darling Harbour wharf and came to under the bows of a steamer moored there. Clegg hopped out and helped Sadie to land. Carrol followed. Then Pat, and Gibble last.

It was early morning but a city's work had begun. Stevedores were trooping in at the wharf gates and the racket of steam winches made a staccato note in the heavy rumble of waterside traffic. Carrol swayed a moment, fresh from the sea, and not yet at home in earth's ugly noises.

"I suppose there's a telephone on the wharf," said Sadie.

"Yes, come along with me," said Clegg.

They went off along the wharf and Carrol strolled to the gates, waiting Sadie's return.

Gibble waited too, with nothing to wait for. He gazed vacantly about, confused by a terrible discovery.

Space was no longer a prison wall of decks and islands, where if he could not possess Sadie he was sure of being tortured by her. Now she was going to vanish beyond a dream of abasement. . . .

But Pat found the moment propitious to rectify another threat of separation. He came across and clapped Carrol on the back.

"Never say you've forgotten it, Jimmy boy."

"Forgotten what?"

"That fiver you owe me for the tree fell on me over yonder."

Carrol hesitated a moment over the ignoble parsimonies of a civilized life, but he pulled out his pocketbook and parted with the fiver. He hesitated at a request in return, too, before saying in a low tone, and a glance at Gibble in the background:

"Look here, Pat, I want to ask you something. When *did* you get Sadie?"

"Never say you found that out on me."

"I didn't, she told me herself."

"Well, and isn't that like a woman too, after swearin' in the breath of me life I'd never mention it? When was it, says you? Why, the day the queer feller has her near out of her mind nosin' after her. I run him off the beach for it, an' she went limp as a rag in me hands. Done up she was, or maybe it was an unbeknownst trick to herself for not knowin' what she is doin'. Sure I petted her like a baby and well she needed it. I guessed at the time what is troublin' her. And I guessed afterwards the way she has of puttin'

it right.   And right she put it, for I had it ready in me mind to knock the heads off you and the queer feller if ever she give me the word to do it."

Carrol swallowed comment on this interesting disclosure because Sadie had come to the wharf gates with Clegg.   They stood there talking earnestly a moment and Carrol heard Sadie say: "It's a nuisance, but as mother's in Melbourne I'll have to go to her.   But I won't be more than a week and I'll send you a wire the moment I'm back."

"Right you are, Sadie."

"Good-by till then, Billy."

She kissed him.   Clegg called, "See you later, Carrol," waved and went down the wharf and Sadie came across to Carrol.

"I rang up my people; got Fanny, fortunately.   She had hysterics at the sound of my voice, so that's all right.   I told her we were coming out straight away. Call a taxi."

Carrol signalled a yellow cab further along the street entrance to the wharf.   It drew up to them and Sadie got in.   Carrol would have followed, but a grip on his coat pulled him back.

"A minute, now," said Pat.   "You're not goin' off without a word in reason and a good-by in season and a hand of friendship passed to one and all."

"All right, good-by," said Carrol impatiently.

"Good-by it is and right it is and here's the word I have to say to you, Jimmy boy.   The grandest girl ever trod in shoe leather you have for wife.   Never deny it—I see the pride of it in your eye this minute. It's you has won the trick, and that's your luck, or else your cunnin', I misdoubt which."

"Oh, go to hell," pished Carrol.

"To hell I'll go and welcome, but for one thing more I have in mind to ask. Sadie dear, will you look me in the eye a minute? Since all is out and ill feelin's done with, answer me this. If you had the startin's of it all over again on the island, and trouble to come at the end of it, which of us three would you pick for the man to see you through with it?"

"You," said Sadie, with magnificent indifference.

"I knew it," said Pat.

"Coogee, driver," yelled Carrol in a fury.

The car started, Pat waved, a groan burst from Gibble but Sadie looked at neither and the car turned its back on them and went away for ever.